D-DAY DOG

ALSO BY TOM PALMER

Scrum
Ghost Stadium
Secret FC

Rugby Academy: Combat Zone
Rugby Academy: Surface to Air
Rugby Academy: Deadlocked

Wings: Flyboy
Wings: Spitfire
Wings: Typhoon

Defenders: Killing Ground
Defenders: Dark Arena
Defenders: Pitch Invasion

Armistice Runner
Over the Line

D-DAY DOG

TOM PALMER

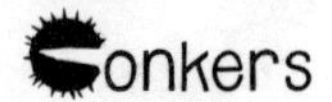

First published in 2019 in Great Britain by
Barrington Stoke Ltd
18 Walker Street, Edinburgh, EH3 7LP

www.barringtonstoke.co.uk

A CIP catalogue record for this book is available from the British Library upon request

ISBN: 978-1-78112-868-8

Printed and bound by CPI Group (UK) Ltd, Croydon, CR0 4YY

For Ashville College, Harrogate,
who kindly took me on their Normandy
school trip, making this book possible

PART 1

ONE

Jack threw the tennis ball and watched it arc over the washing line to bounce at the far edge of the lawn. He grinned as a blur of black and white fur snatched the ball out of the air.

"Good boy, Finn. Now, fetch it."

Finn turned, ball in mouth, scampering to where Jack was crouching. The dog released the ball at the boy's feet, then sat quivering, waiting for Jack to throw it again.

"Good boy," Jack said again, staring into his dog's eager eyes.

Jack had wanted a dog all his life. He had

nagged his mum and dad month on month, year on year. And then – this February – they'd said yes.

"But you have to feed it," Mum cautioned. "You have to walk it. You have to train it. It's your dog. It means less time gaming. Can you cope with that?"

"I can. I will. I promise," Jack had gasped.

And now he'd seen that promise through. Three walks a day. Three meals a day. He'd house-trained Finn. He'd encouraged him to sleep in his crate all night without barking. And now Finn could chase a ball, bring it back and give it up.

The next thing Jack wanted to try was taking Finn out on the pavements and into town without his lead, controlling him with words, not force. But he knew that would be harder, that they would have to build up to it slowly. Jack just wished he didn't have to go back to school and leave his dog at home now the Easter holidays were nearly over.

"Good boy, Finn," Jack praised him a third time.

Then a voice came from the house. Jack and Finn looked up from their game.

"It's here." Dad was standing in front of the open patio doors. "The D-Day game; it's come, Jack. It's time for us to liberate Europe."

Jack and Finn ran towards the house. Dad had been away all weekend training with the Army Reserves, something he did several weekends a year, making Jack extremely proud. His dad was a soldier! And now that he was home, Dad would be able to tell Jack everything he'd been up to.

But first they had a new video game to play.

TWO

"So what do you know about D-Day?" Dad asked.

They were all inside the house now. The front-room lights were on as the sky darkened outside. Father and son perched on the edge of the sofa, controllers in hand, the large-screen TV flashing and droning. Finn was on the sofa too, leaning into Jack, his head resting on the eleven-year-old boy's arm.

Jack shrugged. "What do I know about D-Day?" he answered. "Not a lot."

"I thought you were doing it at school," Dad said. "I mean, your residential trip to Normandy is coming up soon."

"We *are* doing it. We start properly this week with Mr Salah," Jack told him.

Dad took the controller off Jack. "Right," he said. "So, it's important to know about the history that your trip and this game are based on."

"OK," Jack conceded.

Dad faced Jack, rubbing his chin. "So, first things first, D-Day was one of the greatest moments in the history of Europe. You with me so far?"

"Yeah." Jack nodded.

"It took place on 6 June 1944."

"OK."

"And it was one of our finest hours because we – the British – began the liberation of Europe from Nazi Germany." Dad paused. "What do you know about Nazi Germany?"

"Hitler," Jack said.

"Yes. Good. And what did Hitler do?"

"He invaded Europe. He killed millions of people. Or made them his slaves," Jack said.

Dad was nodding. "Not bad. But what about us? In Britain? Did he invade us?"

"His planes bombed us," Jack said. "But he couldn't beat us. The RAF fought back and we won the Battle of Britain with our Spitfire and Hurricane planes."

"That's right." Jack could see his dad was pleased. "Excellent. So now we get to D-Day. What happened next?"

"We invaded them?"

"That's good, Jack. Yes. But not just us. We had a lot of help from the Americans and the Canadians – and soldiers from all over the world. Together, we were called the Allies. Our job was to drive the Germans back and liberate France. It was a massive operation. Over a hundred and fifty thousand men ..."

Jack smiled. His dad was animated again, excited about war and telling Jack about it.

"How do you know all this?" Jack interrupted after a couple of minutes.

"*My* dad," Dad said simply.

Jack noticed the hairs on his dad's arm stand up. It was funny. That always happened when Dad talked about war and *his* dad.

"So, did he tell you all this?" Jack asked.

"Sort of ..." Dad paused. "Well, you know he died when I was seven?"

"Yeah."

"Well, one of the very few things I remember about him was how I used to sit in a massive armchair with him on Sunday afternoons and watch war films. I was brought up knowing all this. And for years after he died, every Sunday I still watched those films ..."

Jack enjoyed hearing his dad talking about Grandad, but today he was desperate to try out the new game, so he was delighted when his dad turned back to the screen and said, "Anyway, on with the game …"

THREE

"You've got to imagine we're two British paratroopers – twenty, maybe twenty-five years old," Dad explained to Jack.

"OK."

"And we're about to jump out of a plane to parachute into the dark and take the fight to the Germans. This is where the liberation of Europe begins. With you and me. We're going to risk our lives to make the world a better place for people who need our help in France, Holland, Belgium and beyond. Do you understand?"

"Yes." Jack really wanted to get started.

"So, are you ready?"

"I'm ready!"

And now they played. Jack and his dad watched dozens of planes taking off from a long dark runway among silhouettes of trees and bushes. The roar of engines filled the room, making Finn look up and stare at Jack intensely.

Next, they were inside a plane, sitting with their backs against the fuselage. Twelve men, their anxious faces smeared with boot polish.

Dad continued his commentary. "So, it's early on 6 June 1944 and hundreds of planes have set off to parachute drop thousands of men into Normandy on the north coast of France. We're on board with them, Jack. Warships and aeroplanes have been bombing the French coastline for weeks, softening up the Germans who had captured the French towns and villages on the coast."

Jack breathed in sharply. He had a question about the towns and villages.

"So had all the French people who lived there before gone away to safety? To get away from the bombs?"

Dad shook his head. "No. Lots of Frenchmen – and some women – fought back against the Nazis that night, sabotaging the German defences to make it easier for the Allies when we arrived. The French were very brave. They knew they had to risk their lives to save their country."

"And what about the ordinary people who didn't fight? Like children my age?" asked Jack. "What happened to them when the bombs fell?"

Dad paused the game and faced Jack for a second time.

"Lots of people were killed, Jack," Dad said in a softer voice. "Hundreds of French people, including children, died that night." Dad coughed. "It's called collateral damage."

"Eh?" Jack had never heard this phrase before.

"When some people die while the army is trying to save everybody else," his dad explained.

"That's a weird name."

Dad nodded. "I suppose it is."

Jack pressed the start button and the screen changed to show a grey sea filled with the silhouettes of hundreds of ships.

"So," Dad went on. "Below us, tens of thousands of men are in ships, ready to storm the beaches. But we're paratroopers. We fly over the enemy, then parachute down to attack them."

Jack concentrated on his game character. He wondered about jumping from a plane, landing in enemy-controlled territory. How would that feel?

Then he thought about his dad. Maybe he'd

already parachuted with the Reserves.

"Have *you* done it?" Jack asked.

Dad was hunched forward, studying the screen. A red light had come on above the open door at the back of the plane.

"Done what?" Dad asked. "Listen, Jack, be ready to jump. That red light means we need to be prepared. When it goes green, we go. OK?"

"Parachuted?" Jack persisted. "Have you ever parachuted? In the Reserves, I mean."

Dad smiled. "I wish … I'd love to. But I've never done that. Some of my mates have done a course. But not me. Not yet."

Jack noticed that the green light had come on in the game.

"Green," he said.

"Well spotted," Dad said. "Follow me."

Jack watched his dad's character fall out of the

doorway into the night, his parachute opening up as he was dragged quickly into the slipstream of the plane. Then Jack made his character jump, the noise and lights of small explosions and lines of orange bullets filling the void around him.

"Now we just drop and hope we don't get hit by German fire," Dad said, breathless, as if he really was falling out of the sky and into a war zone.

Jack felt his legs tense as he watched his character drift down to land. And in the time it took, Jack wondered if one day his dad would do this for real, and he felt a flush of pride about his dad being a Reserve soldier. But with loud bangs crashing around him, he snapped out of it quickly. He heard the sound of another paratrooper crying out in pain. More flashes of bright white light. More ear-splitting cracks and bangs.

Suddenly – back in the real world – Finn was on

his feet, alarmed by the noise, looking around the room, then scampering to hide under a table.

Dad was standing up. “Get ready to hit the ground,” he said. “There could be Germans hiding in those hedgerows, waiting. Look – can you see them?”

Jack nodded, his teeth clamped shut, leaning so far forward that eventually he was standing like his dad.

“I’m ready,” he said.

FOUR

Later that evening, Dad was putting Jack to bed and Finn jumped up to lie on the duvet at his feet. Jack's room was small. His parents called it the box room. But Jack was glad to have a bedroom to himself, with his own posters on the walls, his own games under the bed and a bookcase of his own books. Some of his friends had to share bedrooms with their siblings. Jack would have hated that.

Dad was telling him about his weekend with the Reserves: "... this last time we did night manoeuvres. We were using live rounds – that's real bullets – in the dark."

Jack couldn't get enough of hearing his dad talk about the weapons he'd used and the vehicles he'd been in, including helicopters.

"Up all night on Salisbury Plain," Dad went on. "It was amazing. Every sixth round is a tracer. That means the round lights up, like the ones we saw on the D-Day game. So you can see what you're shooting at and it's easier to hit targets. It was proper full-on training."

"Why did they let you do that, then?" Jack asked, noticing Mum going past his bedroom door.

Dad lowered his voice. He put his hand on Jack's shoulder, making Finn sit up and look quizzically at them. "I've not said yet," Dad explained. "But this morning we were told we're going to be mobilised. I've got a letter about it in my kit."

"What does mobilised mean?"

"It means we have to prepare to go to a warzone."

"Oh wow!" Jack was thrilled. "Where? When?"

"Shhhh," Dad said. "I've not told your mum yet."

"But who will you be fighting?" Jack wasn't listening to his dad's warning, too keen to know what was going to happen. "Will you get to shoot at people?"

"Seriously, Jack," Dad whispered, glancing at the half-closed door. "Shtum. I need to raise it with your mum, choose a good time. You know ..."

Dad went quiet when Jack's mum appeared in the doorway. "Right," she said. "Bedtime. All three of you. And you know Finn's not allowed in your room this late."

Jack rubbed his dog's head. "Bedtime, Finn."

Dad stood up. "I'll take him down," he said.

Finn eyed Jack, then jumped off the bed and trotted into the hallway after Dad.

"Night," Jack called out.

“Night, mate,” Dad’s voice came back as Mum leaned over Jack and straightened the duvet cover, brushing the dog hairs away.

“That dog does everything you say,” Mum said in a quiet voice.

“He’s good,” Jack agreed.

“He is.” Mum smiled. “You’ve worked hard training him; I’m proud of you. You did what you said you’d do. But it’s back to school tomorrow, so you need your sleep.”

“Yes, Mum.”

Mum kissed Jack on the top of his head and switched his bedroom light off, leaving her son staring into the darkness around him, imagining he was on night manoeuvres with his dad, carrying a machine gun, firing tracer bullets at imaginary enemies through his bedroom curtains. He shivered. His dad was going to fight for his country. His dad was going to be in a real war, shooting guns, flying in aeroplanes, maybe even parachuting.

Jack couldn't have been more proud.

FIVE

"So, we've learned that D-Day was the biggest seaborne military invasion ever. Thousands of men dropping out of planes. Tens of thousands coming from ships onto beaches. But why?" Mr Salah asked. "Why did they do it?"

All the blinds were drawn in 6A's classroom, the sun already overheating thirty children just back from the Easter holidays. Two electric fans were humming at the back of the room.

Jack sat where he always sat – with Lucas and Lucas's support teacher, Miss Khan. Jack and Lucas were best friends; they had been since nursery. Lucas insisted Jack sit with him. And that was fine with Jack. Lucas struggled a bit with school and with some of the other children, but together Jack and Miss Khan made sure Lucas could cope. Miss Khan called them "Team Lucas". They were so much of a team that when his dad got Jack a camouflage pencil case, Lucas wasn't happy until he had one of his own. So now they had matching military pencil cases. And Jack and Lucas loved playing war games together, often connecting online over their PlayStations after school.

Mr Salah repeated his question. "Hands up. Who can remember why the Allies invaded France on D-Day?"

"To beat the Germans," Grace Yeboah replied.

"Correct," Mr Salah said. "But what were the Germans doing that we didn't like?"

"Had they invaded France and other countries?" Asma Malik asked.

"Yes. And?"

"And they were doing the Holocaust and killing lots of people," Grace added.

"Yes. Good. Very good."

Jack had his hand up almost constantly as Grace and Asma answered Mr Salah's questions. But his teacher had overlooked him so far.

"And what do you think the Allies did to prepare for the assault?" Mr Salah asked.

Jack stared hard into Mr Salah's eyes now, like Finn stared into his eyes when he wanted something. He knew the answer to this one. He was desperate for his teacher to choose him.

"Jack?" Mr Salah said, noticing him at last.

"The British and Americans bombed France for days to soften the Germans up," Jack said. "They smashed the whole coast to pieces to make it easier for the Allies. Hundreds of people were killed.

Germans. But French people died too. Their houses were blown to pieces, but it was—"

"Very good. But that's enough detail, thanks, Jack," Mr Salah said, glancing at Kasandra Hemsani.

Before Kasandra joined the school in September, Jack's class and 6B had had a lesson where Mr Salah explained that Kasandra was a refugee from Syria. Syria was an ancient country in the Middle East that had been suffering from civil war for years. Half of its population had been forced to leave the country to escape danger on their own streets. Mr Salah had warned them that Kasandra might be very upset about what had happened in Syria, and he warned them to be careful when they talked about D-Day because of that.

"But ..." Jack tried again. He wanted to explain how brave the French people had been, not talk about them being victims.

"He doesn't want you to go on about it," Lucas whispered loudly to Jack so that everyone in the class could hear. Then he turned to look at the teacher. "He's thinking about Kasandra and how she had to leave Syria and how her house was probably blown to pieces too, but that she's never told anyone anything about it, so no one knows for sure. I've asked her, sir, but she—"

"Lucas," Mr Salah said. "Do you want to stop, please?"

"No, sir," Lucas said. "I don't."

Jack watched Miss Khan try to make eye contact with Lucas, to warn him to be quiet.

"Well, I think you should stop, Lucas," said Mr Salah.

With Lucas silenced, Jack took his chance to explain.

"But the French wanted rid of the Germans

even more than we did," Jack weighed in. "If they had to deal with a few bombs falling in their back gardens, they'd take it."

"Idiot!" Grace snapped.

"Yeah, think about it, Jack," Grace's friend, Ella Smith, added.

Mr Salah stepped forward with his hand up. All of 6A knew that gesture meant: *Stop talking. Silence. Listen to me.*

The whole class did what was expected of them. Mr Salah waited for a few seconds.

"He's going to tell us off now," Lucas whispered loudly.

A wave of laughter rippled around the room. Jack noticed Kasandra was smiling too.

"No," Mr Salah said. "I'm not going to tell you all off, Lucas. What we've got here is a disagreement. Can we agree on that, at least?"

6A said, "Yes."

"Let's think about it," Mr Salah said. "Disagreeing is normal. We are all different. We all see the world in different ways. Some of us think war is exciting. Some of us think it is frightening. Some of us have never thought about it or talked about it before. But what we need to do is agree to *disagree* and to always hear each other out. And *not* – Grace and Ella – call each other names."

"But Jack—" Grace complained.

"But Jack what?" Mr Salah said. "If Jack thinks it is OK that one part of France was bombed so that the rest of France could be liberated, then we have to listen. This is something that can happen in wartime. When people are killed by those who are actually on their side, it's called collateral damage. Often it happens by accident, but sometimes a decision is made to strike a target even when there is a chance that innocent people will be killed."

Mr Salah looked at Jack. "But we have to hear Grace out too. Grace, tell Jack why you think what he said is wrong. But do it in a nice way, please."

Grace looked at Kasandra, then shrugged at her teacher; she was reluctant to speak now.

Mr Salah lowered his head and sighed. "I think we should leave it for today," he said. "Soon we will be heading to Normandy with 6B for our D-Day residential. We will visit inspiring places including Pegasus Bridge, where British soldiers landed in gliders to take the Germans by surprise; and Omaha Beach, where American soldiers arrived on ships and waded out of the waves; and, finally, Ranville Cemetery, where many British dead were buried. So, we have some more time to explore these issues." Mr Salah surveyed 6A and said, "That's kind of the point, you know, of us learning all this history and talking about it before we go to France. So we can really understand what happened during the Second World War and work out how we feel about it."

The lesson was over. Jack grinned. He knew what he was going to do tonight. He was going to ask his dad about the places Mr Salah had mentioned. Pegasus Bridge. Omaha Beach. Ranville Cemetery. He had written them down, even more excited about the trip now.

SIX

After school, Jack took Finn for a walk along the side of the river near to where they lived. The river was deep and slow moving.

Along the banks there were signs that summer was coming: green shoots forcing themselves out of the ground and from the tips of the branches of trees. A bank of bluebells on the far side of the river. The noise of birds chattering.

Jack let Finn run frantically up and down the riverbank, then dive in after a stick at least twenty times. Jack knew this would tire Finn out, so that when Dad got home from work they could play the

D-Day game without worrying about him. A tired dog was a happy dog.

Finn jumped in after the stick, emerging each time dripping with water, scampering up to Jack and dropping the stick at his feet. Jack knew not to take the stick immediately. He'd step back and watch Finn shake the water out of his coat. Then Finn would stare at Jack, urging him to throw it again.

Jack was learning how important eye contact was between him and his dog. It was like they could read each other's minds with just a glance. When it was time to go home, Jack didn't even need to tell Finn that he wasn't going to throw the stick again. One look at Jack as he came out of the water and Finn knew.

Jack checked the time on his phone. Dad would be back by now.

"Time to liberate Europe," Jack said to Finn, then dog and boy walked home together.

*

Dad's car was parked on the street at the front of the house when they arrived home. Excited, Jack let Finn into the garden, shut the wooden gate behind him and was about to head into the house when he noticed that Finn was waiting by the open front door instead of rushing in like he normally did.

"What's up, Finn?"

Then Jack heard shouting. An argument. A loud one. Mum and Dad. Jack decided to join Finn on the doorstep to sit it out. He put his arm around his dog, moved two empty milk bottles from the edge of the doorstep and listened.

"I can't believe you looked at my letter." Dad's voice.

"I can't believe *you've* been hiding this from us." Mum was shouting.

"It was addressed to me. It was in my kit."

"Which is the worst crime, Rob? Me reading a letter in your bag? Or you going to fight in a war without telling me?"

Jack heard no reply from his dad.

"So, now I know about it, can I ask some questions?"

"Sure," Dad said defensively. "If you want to."

"I do want to."

"Fine."

"Thank you." Mum was no longer shouting, but her voice was still seething with fury. "When are you meant to be going?" she asked.

"We mobilise in July," Dad replied. "Probably deploy in the late autumn."

"Where?"

"Afghan."

"That's Afghanistan, yeah?" Mum paused. "Where over 400 British soldiers have died since we got ourselves mixed up in their ..." Mum used a swear word at this point.

Dad remained silent.

Jack heard a rustling sound and then his dad saying, "That's helpful."

"What, Rob?" Mum snapped back. "Me throwing a screwed-up piece of paper at you is helpful, is it? Is it more helpful than a hand grenade? How about I throw one of them at you? I feel like you've thrown one at me."

"Love ..." Dad said.

"Love?" Mum shouted. "Don't call me love. What do you think love is?" Mum's voice was breaking up now. Jack could tell she was close to tears.

"It's what *we* have," Dad said. Jack noticed that Dad's voice was meek now.

"*Love*, Rob, in this house, is about you and me working together as a couple, making joint decisions and doing our best for Jack, not you going off on your own and making a decision that will send shockwaves through his world. And mine."

"He's pleased," Dad said.

Another silence.

Jack closed his eyes. He could tell that his dad had made a mistake by the fact Mum was no longer talking. One thing Jack had learned about Mum was that so long as she was talking – even shouting – there was hope. It was when she was silent that there was real trouble.

"What?" Mum asked.

Dad's voice was weak. "Jack's pleased."

"You told him?"

"I—"

"You told him last night," Mum interrupted, "when I came in and you took Finn away. I don't believe this, Rob! You told Jack before you talked it through with me? Of course he was pleased. He loves you. He worships you. If you do something, it's the best thing in the world. But do you really think he'll still be pleased the next time he sees on the news that some British Army soldiers have driven over a landmine and been blown up?"

No answer.

"Well?"

"I don't know," Dad mumbled.

"Think about it, Rob."

More silence.

"So why?" Mum pressed.

"Why what?"

"Why did you keep it a secret from me? Because you were scared I wouldn't want to let you go? Is that it?"

"YEAH!" Dad was shouting now. "To be honest. Yeah!"

Jack had been expecting this. Dad shouting. But he also knew that Dad shouting never lasted long. Jack waited, restraining Finn as he heard his mum crying now, his dad talking to her in a low and soft voice, then him crying too. Jack was desperate to hear what they were saying, but he couldn't.

He had heard them argue before. Parents argued; that was normal.

But there was something different about their argument this time.

Maybe it was because Jack was older now and he understood that Dad really wanted one thing and Mum really wanted another, which meant that if things were going to get better, one of them was going to have to give in.

Jack couldn't see either of them giving in.

So, what would happen? Were things *not* going to get better?

Jack had seen enough of his friends' parents split up to know divorce happened. A lot. Was that going to happen to his parents? And then what would happen to Jack and Finn?

SEVEN

The next day there was a buzz in the school IT suite. Every child sat at a screen with a keyboard in front of them. Most of them were watching Mr Salah, who, in turn, was studying Lucas.

Mr Salah breathed in. "Lucas? Why are you typing already?"

Normally Jack would have tried to stop Lucas, but he was too distracted, still thinking about his mum and dad, last night, the argument.

"I'm working," Lucas informed Mr Salah.

"But the screens aren't switched on yet, Lucas."

"I know, sir. I'm bored, sir." Lucas grinned.

"But ... oh, forget it. Let's move on, shall we?" Mr Salah took a sip from his cup of tea. "Today," he said, "is the day we begin our Normandy projects."

Most of 6A let out an eager cheer. But not Jack. Jack just looked around him. He didn't feel like cheering today.

"Why do we need the computers, sir?" Ella asked.

"Good question, Ella. Well, we want to make this residential trip as meaningful to you as possible. We want you to have a personal connection with what we are doing and where we are going. So, we are going to ask you to choose someone who died on D-Day and research their story. Someone who is buried in the cemetery we are visiting at Ranville, so that you can plant one of these crosses at the end of the trip."

Mr Salah held up a small wooden cross with a red poppy at its centre.

"How do we choose?" Grace asked as the rest of the class looked eagerly at Mr Salah.

"Another good question, Grace. You might have the same surname as them. You might have been born in the same place as them. There might be something you like about what they did. Have a look at the details of the soldiers who are buried in Ranville Cemetery. See if you can find a connection with one. There's a website listing everyone buried in the village."

6A settled down to do their research.

*

"OK," Mr Salah said twenty minutes later. "How are we doing? Who'd like to start us off?"

The teacher was standing in the centre of the room.

Jack had been busy. He'd found things that excited him and he was feeling a bit happier now. He thrust his hand up first, staring directly into his teacher's eyes.

"Jack?"

"I've found Stan Hollis. He won the Victoria Cross. The men who won the Victoria Cross were the bravest. He killed loads of Germans when he stormed their bunker and dropped a grenade inside to blow them to pieces so that the rest of his men survived under fire. Then he caught eighteen more Germans on the beach and took them prisoner."

"Thank you, Jack. Stan Hollis sounds a remarkable man," Mr Salah said. "Is he buried in Ranville Cemetery?"

"No," Jack explained. "He didn't die. He survived."

"Did you find Stan Hollis on the website I asked you to look at, Jack?"

"No, sir."

"OK. We were supposed to be searching for people who were buried in Ranville Cemetery. We might need to work on that, Jack? I'd like you to choose someone whose grave you can visit on our trip. Who wants to go next?"

More hands shot up, others telling the class whom they had chosen.

Lucas had chosen a very young soldier called Robert Johns, who had been only sixteen when he was killed. Jack felt more and more disappointed that Stan Hollis didn't count. Some of the soldiers the other children were choosing hadn't done nearly as much as Stan.

The last to speak was Kasandra.

"I would like to choose a girl," she said.

Jack leaned forward. *A girl?* he thought. He'd had enough. *There were no girls involved in D-Day.*

"Do you want to tell us about her?" Mr Salah said softly. "What was her name?"

"She was called Myriam," Kasandra said. "She lived in one of the houses in Ranville. And she is buried in the village. Not in the war cemetery, but in the Ranville churchyard, next to it."

Jack felt his feet press on the floor – he was going to stand up.

"The village was bombed and she died," Kasandra said quietly.

Jack was standing now. "Sir, she can't choose a civilian. Civilians don't count. We're meant to be learning about soldiers, not collateral damage."

Mr Salah narrowed his eyes and stared at Jack.

No one spoke. For a long time. Jack could hear the clock ticking. He looked at Miss Khan – she was shaking her head.

Jack knew he'd said something wrong. He

wished he could take it back, but he felt so cross about everything today after listening to his parents arguing last night.

At last Mr Salah spoke. "That was not acceptable, Jack. Have you thought about why Kasandra chose who she chose?"

"No," Jack said meekly. He knew he'd been horrible. But it was done.

Mr Salah was standing over Jack, his hands on the desk in front of him.

"Maybe you should."

"Sir?" Lucas was standing up now too.

"Not now, Lucas," Mr Salah said.

"But, I ... I think I know why Kasandra—"

"Not now, Lucas, please. Jack, come with me."

EIGHT

Outside in the corridor, Mr Salah knelt on the carpeted floor to be eye-to-eye with Jack. Jack was staring at a display on the wall outside one of the Year 4 classrooms. They were doing the Romans.

"Can you look at me, please, Jack?" his teacher asked. "I need you to know that I cannot allow you to treat Kasandra like that. It's mean ..."

"I wasn't—"

"You were, Jack. You were trying to make her change her mind about who she should choose. Have you forgotten the time we spent learning about Syria before Kasandra joined us?"

"No, sir."

"Her city was bombed and thousands of people were killed. Her parents had to leave everything they owned and escape with their children. But we don't know the details of what happened to Kasandra and her family. Like Lucas said, she has not shared that with anyone yet. She is here with her mum. That's all we know and we have to be sensitive to that. You think that war is exciting because you are interested in guns and soldiers. And that's fine. But you also have to think about the people who get caught in the crossfire. Like Kasandra. And about using phrases like collateral damage."

"But you told us about collateral damage, sir," Jack objected.

"Maybe I did, but you are missing the point, Jack. Again. I will not tolerate you saying things like that. Do you understand?"

Jack swallowed. He knew he'd been unkind to Kasandra. He could feel tears forming in his eyes. This was all too much. "Yes, sir. I'm sorry, sir."

"You will need to find a way to apologise to Kasandra too, Jack. And if anything like that happens again, I will have to reconsider if I want you to come to France. Is that clear?"

Jack felt a rush of heat in his throat and chest. He breathed in quickly. He glanced into the classroom and saw Lucas staring at him, a frown forming on his face.

"Yes, sir," he muttered.

Mr Salah paused. "Is everything all right with you, Jack? You seem a bit off today."

"I'm fine, sir."

"Your new dog? Is he OK?"

"He's fine, sir," Jack said. Jack was pleased Mr Salah had remembered he had a dog. His mind turned to Finn now. To going home and being with Finn.

Finn was great.

Finn always made him feel better.

NINE

"How was school?" Mum asked.

"Fine," Jack muttered.

They were in the kitchen after Jack had taken Finn for a walk. Mum was dismantling the extractor fan above the cooker. Bits of metal and screws covered half the kitchen table. Jack was doing his Maths homework on the other half. He wanted to ask Mum about Dad. About what they had been saying to each other.

Jack glanced at Mum. She was studying him, pointing a screwdriver at him.

"Are you OK, Jack?"

Jack shrugged.

"Really?" Mum said. "You don't seem yourself."

Jack took a sip from his glass of juice. He had a question.

"Where's Dad?"

Mum hesitated. "He's staying at your gran's tonight."

"But he's coming back?" Jack didn't like this news. He was doubly worried now.

"Yes, of course," Mum said.

"I heard you arguing yesterday."

"I see."

Mum had stepped back and Jack could see she didn't know what to say.

"Are you going to stop him from going to war?" Jack asked.

Mum stepped forward again and put down the screwdriver. She eyed Jack.

Finn sat up in his crate and sighed.

"It's not ... I mean ..." Mum looked stuck for words. Then she nodded. "Shall I be honest?"

"If you like," Jack said.

"I really don't want him to go to Afghanistan. So ... well ... yes, I'm going to do everything I can to stop him."

Jack pushed his Maths homework across the table. "But that's not fair."

"Isn't it?" Mum asked.

"No."

"On who? Who's it not fair on, Jack?"

"Dad."

"Yeah, but it's not just about Dad, is it?" Mum had her hands on her hips.

"Eh?"

"He's my husband," Mum said as Finn stood up suddenly, looking at the kitchen door. "He's your dad.

He's your gran's son. If you get married and have children, you have a duty to your family ..."

"He's got a duty to the army," Jack said loudly. "He's got a duty to the country."

Mum shook her head. Her face looked hard. "Not above his duty to me and you, he doesn't," she said.

Jack noticed that Finn was wagging his tail, eyes on the door. But for once Jack ignored what his dog was trying to tell him.

"Yes, he does," Jack said. "He's a soldier. That comes first."

Mum sat down and stared at Jack. "It does not. His family should be more important to him than anything else."

"That's stupid," Jack said. "You're mad if you think anything means more to him than the army."

"You're wrong," Dad said. The door had clicked open.

Jack swung round. Mum too. Dad was in the doorway.

"I thought you were staying at your mum's?" Mum said, confused.

"I've come for some things," Dad answered.

"Right."

Dad knelt next to Jack, keeping Finn away by stroking the dog's head and ears.

"What you said about the army," Dad said. "It's wrong. You and Mum are more important to me than the army."

"No, we're not," Jack protested.

"Of course you are."

Jack didn't know what to think or say. "So why are you staying at Gran's?"

"I need to work things out in my head," Dad explained. "I'm sorry. It's not an easy thing to think about at home."

Jack shrugged. He looked at his mum. She said nothing.

"A few days. That's all," Dad said. "But I need you to promise me something when I'm not here."

Jack kept looking at Dad.

"Will you promise?"

"I don't know what it is yet," Jack said.

Dad smiled. "Don't blame your mum for this. It's not her fault. She's looking out for you."

Jack shrugged again, then stared at the screws and tools on the table. At that moment his stomach felt like it was full of screws and tools. Really heavy and painful. He felt like he didn't have any energy. Certainly not enough energy to blame anyone for anything.

TEN

At bedtime Jack heard Mum coming upstairs.

"Finn," Jack said. "Bedtime."

Finn jumped off the bed, ready to go to his crate in the kitchen. Mum smiled. Her eyes were red. "You two are a good team," she said.

"Finn, kitchen now," Jack said.

"I was wondering ..." Mum said, grabbing the dog's collar as he went past, "if you'd like him up here with you tonight?"

"Yeah?" Jack grinned.

"Yeah."

Jack patted the bed. "Up, Finn."

Finn didn't need to be told twice. He leaped onto the bed and settled down at Jack's feet, his dark brown eyes studying Mum.

"I'm shattered," Mum said. "I've locked up. I'm sorry about today. It's complicated. But you don't need to worry about things, OK? We'll sort this out, once your dad has got his head round it."

"OK, Mum," Jack said.

"I need to ask you about something else too," Mum went on. "Lucas's mum called me. She said he was worried about Normandy and wanted to check you were still going. I said you were and that there's nothing wrong. He said something happened at school today?"

Jack frowned. "I got told off. I said something stupid. That's all. But it's OK. Nothing to worry about. Lucas thinks an argument means it's the end of the world. I'll talk to him tomorrow."

"Good lad. You're kind to Lucas. I'm proud of you for that. Do we need to talk about what happened at school?"

"It's fine," Jack said.

"OK. I'll see you in the morning." Mum bent down to kiss Jack's head. She patted Finn, then switched the light out.

"Night, boys," Mum said.

"Night, Mum," Jack replied, then gently pulled Finn up the bed so his head was on the pillow.

"This is all right, Finn." Jack grinned to his dog, seeing his outline in the almost-dark of the room. Jack noticed that Finn's ears were down, his eyes mournful. And Jack suddenly understood that Finn being in his bedroom was not a good thing. It was his mum's way of trying to comfort him about his dad being gone.

ELEVEN

Back in the IT suite the next morning, Jack went straight over to Lucas and talked about what they'd do in Normandy together. He wanted to make sure his friend felt good about the trip. When Lucas grinned, Jack knew he'd reassured him.

After he'd finished talking to Lucas, Jack saw that the only computer free was next to Kasandra. It was a good chance to talk to her too.

"Hi," Jack said, sitting down.

"Hi."

"I'm sorry about what I said yesterday," Jack said.

"It's OK." Kasandra smiled.

But even though he had done his best to talk to Lucas, then Kasandra, Jack still felt sad. Sad about home.

"OK, 6A," Mr Salah said, beginning the lesson. "I want you to go back online now and discover more about the soldier or civilian you've been researching. See if you can find any other sources that will give you more information than the internet. Books, for instance. The internet is great, but you need other sources too."

After addressing the whole class, Mr Salah came to squat between Jack and Kasandra.

"Jack?"

"Sir."

"Dogs."

"Sorry, sir?"

"I've been doing a bit of reading that might interest you. Type in 'D-Day' and 'dogs'."

Jack did as he was told and studied the first result at the top of the page:

The Parachuting Dogs of the British Army
Britain's heroic Luftwoofe. The paradogs of the Second World War.

As they prepared for D-Day and the fight against Nazi Germany, the 13th Parachute Battalion of the British Army developed a new weapon: parachuting dogs ...

Jack shuddered. Not at what he was reading. Not exactly. It was something else. He'd had a fleeting image of himself standing at the back entrance of a plane, like the one in the D-Day game, with Finn in his arms gazing up at him with that I-love-you look in his deep brown eyes. Then Jack threw Finn out of the plane and the dog disappeared into the darkness, his yelps fading as he fell.

Jack shook his head, trying to get rid of the horrible image. He could never do that to Finn.

Never.

“Is it a joke, sir?” Jack asked. “You always say that we can’t trust everything we find on the internet.”

“I’m afraid it’s no joke, Jack,” Mr Salah said. “Have a read of a few of these articles. You might find something interesting. Search ‘D-Day dogs’ and some of the places we’re going to. And once you’ve done that, there’s a book at the library in town. It’s called *Animals that Helped Win the War*. I’ve checked the library catalogue online and they have it in stock.”

Mr Salah moved on to speak to Kofi and Danny at the next table.

Jack searched and quickly found more

information about dogs being trained to jump out of aeroplanes on D-Day, so that, once on the ground, they could sniff out minefields and listen out for the enemy before the British soldiers could see or hear them.

He looked for images relating to the places Mr Salah had told them they would be visiting. Pegasus Bridge. Omaha Beach. Ranville.

And then Jack saw the picture.

A German Shepherd dog was staring out of the screen at him. It was tall with huge pointy ears. But even though it was a massive dog, it didn't look frightening. Jack smiled to himself; he felt a bit better now. The dog looked calm and kind. Jack knew that dogs could be kind. Finn was.

"He is a nice dog." Kasandra was leaning towards Jack as she gazed at the image. "He looks strong."

Jack nodded. "Yeah," he said. Then he scrolled down to read more, somehow feeling proud of the dog even though he'd only known about him for seconds.

"I like dogs," Kasandra volunteered. "I had two dogs."

Jack looked at Kasandra. For some reason he hadn't imagined people would have dogs in Syria. He didn't know what to say now. Everyone knew that Kasandra never talked about her home and he was scared of upsetting her. So he said nothing.

Jack looked back at his computer. The dog on the screen was called Glen. Its handler's name was Emile Corteil. Jack made some notes, glancing at Kasandra, who was working on her own project.

Jack cleared the search engine and typed again. "Glen. Emile. Cortiel."

There were no results. Jack frowned. He hated

this about the internet. You search for something and expect to see thousands of articles but then nothing comes up.

He searched again.

Nothing.

Just when he'd thought he might have found something really interesting, he'd lost it. Jack felt frustration run through him. This was too much. His worries about his mum and dad resurfaced. He closed his eyes and felt that sadness creeping over him again.

"It's C-O-R-T-E-I-L." Jack heard Kasandra spell out the name of the man he was searching for on the internet.

"What?" Jack asked.

"That is how you need to spell it."

Jack looked at the screen. Kasandra was right. He'd spelt Corteil wrong.

"Oh yeah ... thanks," Jack said. He looked at Kasandra's screen. He felt like he should keep the conversation going. Maybe he should ask her something about her project now. She had helped him after all.

"Have you found more about your girl?" Jack asked.

Kasandra's face lit up with a broad smile. She pointed to the screen at a photograph of a small girl in a dress, standing next to a tree. There was a French word on a shop front behind her.

"How old was she?" Jack asked.

"Eleven."

"Like us?"

"Yes."

"And she ... was she killed?"

"Yes," Kasandra replied. "Did the dog live?"

"What?"

"Did your dog live?"

Jack understood that Kasandra was changing the subject.

"I don't know yet," Jack said. "I hope so."

Suddenly two arms were thrust between them.

Lucas.

"I bet the dog got blasted to pieces, like your girl," Lucas said, laughing. Then he made a noise that was supposed to sound like an explosion and waved his arms in the air.

Kasandra recoiled, staring at her screen.

Jack felt a hot flash of anger. "It's not funny, Lucas," he said.

Now Lucas was backing away, his voice wobbling. "It is funny, Jack," Lucas said. "It's just like when we play war games on the PlayStation. You laugh then."

Jack shook his head. He didn't really know what to say. He and Lucas did have a laugh when they were playing video games. But this was different.

Miss Khan was with them now. She took Lucas back to his seat.

"Sorry," Jack said to Kasandra when his friend had gone.

Kasandra smiled. "It's OK," she said, then she stared hard at her screen again.

*

At the end of the lesson Jack was still searching the internet. He had found out more about Glen and Emile Corteil. They had trained together for months, learning how to jump out of planes, then meet up on the ground and use the dog's superior senses of smell and hearing to save other soldiers' lives. Their story spoke to Jack: one man and his dog against the world. That was how he felt about himself and Finn.

"Good stuff?" Mr Salah said, interrupting Jack's thoughts. "The class is over. Look. Everyone else has gone on break."

Jack was surprised that he'd missed the bell and the clamour of 6A leaving the room. "Yeah. Thanks, sir," he said. "I'm into this now. I'm going to the library to get that book. So I can find out more."

TWELVE

Jack walked into town to visit the central library the next day. Through the sliding doors, past a smile from a librarian and up the stairs.

He knew his way around the library. His mum and dad had been bringing him here for as long as he could remember. Non-fiction was on the first floor: turn left at the top of the stairs, along the first aisle to History, then two shelves down.

And there it was: the Second World War.

Jack found the small book easily. *Animals that Helped Win the War*. It had a photomontage of animals and birds on the cover. Jack leafed through to see that each page had a few paragraphs with the name of an animal and its photograph at the top. He found pigeons, horses, sheep. Then dogs.

Jack kept going until he saw a picture of Glen, sitting on the ground, his chest puffed out, staring directly into the camera.

Man's Best Friend

Emile Corteil, the son of a French man and a British woman, volunteered to fight in the Second World War when he was eighteen. He trained for a year to be among the fittest and most daring soldiers in the British Army, part of the force that would attack the Nazis from the air.

Emile loved the countryside – perhaps too much, because one night he was caught off his army base, poaching. Soldiers were not allowed to poach and Emile had to be punished by his superior officer.

And what was his punishment?

He was given a dog. A German Shepherd called Glen. Emile's job was to train Glen to be a paradog.

As you might have guessed, for Emile this was no punishment. He loved animals as much as he loved the countryside. He liked dogs in particular. And he came to love Glen more than any other dog.

Glen needed to be able to sniff out explosive mines hidden underground and hear Germans on the battlefield. He had to be able to indicate to Emile what he had sensed.

But Emile also had to train Glen to jump out of aeroplanes from hundreds of metres up in the sky. D-Day would not be possible without paratroopers dropping in behind enemy lines. Human and canine. Emile must have worried about whether Glen would be able to do that. But Glen loved leaping out of planes and drifting back to earth on his parachute, something they did at least a dozen times before the big day.

They trained for more than a year, dog and man learning to communicate with each other, so that Emile could warn his fellow soldiers that Glen had heard or smelled danger. They were a brilliant team and were a key part of the planned attack on an important gun position called the Merville Battery.

But on the day of the drop – 6 June 1944 – Glen was not keen to jump. The noise of the flak around the plane as the Germans fired at them disturbed the dog. When the moment came for the big drop, Glen cowered, trembling, under a bench. Emile and another paratrooper had to pull him out of his hiding place and throw him from the plane.

Some people say that Glen had a premonition about what was going to happen next to him and his master.

Jack swallowed. He had a bad feeling about the last few paragraphs he still had to read about Glen and Emile. In his mind he was again imagining throwing Finn out into the night, with bombs and bullets and tracer fire all around him, Finn cowering from the explosions and cracks of gunfire. Jack imagined the look Finn would give him if he tried to do that. Would Finn still trust him like he did now?

Glen and Emile had done all that training together. They were just like Finn and Jack. A dog and a boy working together, listening to each other, understanding each other.

Jack felt sick. No, he could never do that to his dog. What had made Mr Salah think that him finding out about Glen was a good idea?

Jack rubbed his face.

And what did it mean in the book when it said that Glen had a premonition? A premonition of what?

Jack breathed in deeply. He would read the rest. He had to know what happened.

After the confusion in the aeroplane, the dog and young man landed some distance away from their intended drop zone, along with many other British paratroopers. It meant that for the attack on the Merville Battery to be a success, the men had to move quickly to get to the correct location.

The Merville Battery was a German gun position that could aim huge shells at the beaches where the Allies would be landing later that day. It had to be destroyed or thousands of Allied soldiers would be killed.

Emile and Glen joined up with some other men to march in the dark to the Merville Battery, the skies above them full of sound and fury.

Glen led from the front with Emile beside him,

the dog listening out for the enemy in the fields and hedgerows around them. No doubt he was sniffing the ground to make sure the men did not step on mines.

As Jack read on, his eyes blurred with tears. He knew already that Emile was buried in Ranville Cemetery. But he hadn't really thought about what must have happened to him and Glen. It was too much.

How could Emile Corteil have done that to Glen?

How could he put his dog in such danger, throwing him from a plane and into a warzone?

Jack's mouth felt dry. He coughed, wondering if he was going to be sick. He was disgusted. Disgusted by war. Disgusted by Corteil. Even disgusted by his dad for being so excited about war and making Jack feel the same way.

Well, that was it. Jack didn't think war was exciting any more.

THIRTEEN

When he got home from the library, Jack released Finn from his crate and hugged him. Mum and Dad were not there. And Jack was glad.

"I'd never do that to you," he whispered to his dog as Finn tried to chew Jack's ear.

Once Jack released Finn, the dog sat back and studied him. His brown eyes stared deep into Jack's and Jack peered at his dog.

"What?"

Finn put his head on one side.

"I'm fine."

Finn didn't move.

"Shall we ... go for ... a ... walk?!"

Finn sprinted for the door, glancing back at Jack to check he was grabbing the lead. Finn barked. Jack took two poo bags out of their box. He felt reckless and held the lead out to Finn. "Do we need this?" he asked.

Finn barked.

Jack put the lead in his pocket.

Outside – after he'd locked the door – Jack walked slowly and pointed at his own feet. "Stay with me," he said in a firm voice. Even so, Jack was nervous. This was a big move, taking Finn close to the roads without his lead. He took a dog biscuit out of his pocket and gave it to Finn. "Good boy. Stay with me."

Finn walked alongside Jack, matching his pace, through the garden gate and along the road towards the zebra crossing. Past the noise of cars, a man pushing a pram, and a girl on a skateboard. Finn stayed focused. He didn't miss a stride, even with so many interesting things around him.

But when they reached the zebra crossing, Finn noticed a collie on the other side of the road. The dog glanced at Jack.

"Stay with me, Finn," Jack said. "Sit."

Finn sat and gazed across the zebra crossing as the traffic slowed down and stopped. The collie had sprinted away across the field on the other side.

Jack gave Finn another biscuit.

"Good boy. Very good boy. Stay with me," Jack said, walking slowly over the zebra crossing.

Finn matched Jack step for step.

When they reached the other side of the road and the open field leading to the riverbank ahead – the place where Jack usually let Finn off his lead – Jack said, "Go on. Go on, Finn."

Finn went off like a rocket, in pursuit of the collie.

Jack put his hands on his hips and watched, feeling his hammering heart begin to calm. He couldn't believe the risk he'd just taken, walking Finn across the road off the lead. But it had shown Jack that Finn trusted him – and shown Finn that he could trust Jack.

And that made Jack feel a bit better.

FOURTEEN

"This time next week," Mr Salah began, "we will be in France."

6A cheered, arms in the air, smiles on their faces. Their teacher waited for them to calm down. He was grinning too.

"This time next week, we will be taking our crosses to Ranville Cemetery and paying our respects to our soldiers and the other people we want to remember."

Now there was a round of excited applause, all the children clapping wildly.

Except Jack.

Jack had been thinking hard all night. He had barely slept because he couldn't stop imagining himself pushing Finn out of an aeroplane and the look of betrayal his dog would give him as he fell away into the blackness. Finn had been with him on his bed all night again. A night during which Jack had made a decision.

Jack noticed Mr Salah was watching him, so he put up his hand.

As the class calmed down for a second time, Mr Salah nodded to Jack.

"Jack?"

"Sir, I'm not coming."

"Coming where, Jack?"

"To France."

Gasps.

Shouts.

Questions from around the classroom.

Jack was aware that, next to him, Miss Khan was trying to stop Lucas from standing up.

"Shall we go outside and talk about it, Jack?" Mr Salah said.

"There's no need, sir," Jack said. "I won't change my mind. I hate war. I don't want to go to a place where we have to learn about war and killing."

"That's quite a turnaround, Jack. You say you *hate* war now?" Mr Salah said.

Lucas had broken away from Miss Khan and was walking towards the front of the class. "I'm not coming either, sir," Lucas said.

Some of the children at the back of the class were laughing now.

"Lucas. Please. Keep out of this. You *are* coming. Jack. Can we—"

Jack interrupted his teacher. "I read the book you told me about and you were right when you said we should think about the people caught in the crossfire and that I should think more about war from the point of view of people like Kasandra. I think war is horrible. I don't *want* to talk about it any more. I'm not coming."

"I see," Mr Salah said. "Then, please, can we go on with the lesson and talk about this at break, perhaps?"

Jack nodded, but he was not going to change his mind. He hated war. He used to love it. He used to think it was exciting, even funny. Not now. That was over.

PART 2

FIFTEEN

Jack sat in the passenger seat as his mum drove him the short distance to school. The streets were dark and unfamiliar at midnight. Few cars. Few pedestrians. Not even dog-walkers, it was so late.

Jack held Finn close to his chest. His dog was chewing the sleeves of Jack's blue Normandy tour hoodie. The last thing in the world Jack wanted to do was leave Finn, but he had made a deal. With his dad.

He was going to France.

*

After Jack's announcement a week earlier that he wasn't going on the residential trip, his mum had been called in to school, but even she couldn't persuade him to change his mind.

Then Dad had come back home. To see Jack.

Dad said he needed time to think about whether he would go to Afghanistan. And part of that thinking would involve talking with Mum without having to worry about Jack. They needed to find a way forward together. So they'd asked Jack to go on the trip while they took some time to figure things out.

Jack agreed. What else could he do? He'd wondered about asking, *And what if you can't figure things out?* But he didn't.

Back in school, he'd also reached a deal with Mr Salah.

Jack would be given his cross. But he did not

have to plant it in Ranville Cemetery if he didn't want to. He wouldn't be forced to visit any of the museums or cemeteries either, if he didn't want to go. He could stay on the bus with the coach driver instead.

*

They were closer to school now.

Jack could see light coming from behind the high hedges that surrounded the school playing fields. It looked as if a spaceship had landed on the pitches. But Jack knew it was just cars.

In the car park, headlights caught the faces of some of his classmates, some excited and animated, others not. Jack spotted Kofi with Danny. Then Grace and Asma. Ella. Kasandra.

When Jack saw Lucas – standing with his mum

and Miss Khan, but scanning the car park, his face tense – Jack rolled down the window and called out to his friend. He saw the tension fade and a wide grin appear on Lucas's face.

The car parked up, but Jack didn't move. He could sense that Finn was staring at him in the darkness, but he couldn't bring himself to return the gaze.

Finn knew that Jack was going away. He had sat in the corner of the room as Jack's mum packed his stuff.

"Does Mr Salah know about Dad and all the stuff about Afghanistan?" Jack asked his mum now.

"Yes," Mum replied. "He won't mention it, but he's aware that you need looking out for. Is that OK?"

Jack nodded.

"He's pleased you're coming," Mum went on. "He thinks you're brave."

Jack buried his face in Finn's fur and closed his eyes.

Outside, Jack and Finn followed Mum as she wheeled his suitcase to the back of the bus. Jack held Finn's lead tight. The dog was nervy. He wished he'd left Finn in the car. But it was too late to change his mind now.

They arrived alongside the coach. A short heavy-set man with two armfuls of tattoos and a cigarette in his mouth was loading bags into the large hold between the wheels. Jack assumed he was the driver.

Jack stood with Mum and Finn, watching his classmates, all of them in their blue tour hoodies, waiting for their turn to hand over their bags.

"You want that on the bus?" the driver asked Jack gruffly. "Or are you gonna stand there all night?"

"Thank you," Mum said, pushing Jack's suitcase towards the driver.

Jack decided he didn't like the man.

They moved away from the bus to where Mrs Mace, the head teacher, was standing with a box of plastic folders.

"Evening, Mrs Ashville," she said to Jack's mum. "Are you all set for Normandy, Jack?"

Jack wanted to say no. But he nodded. He felt Finn's nose on his hand. He knelt and put his dog in a headlock and they wrestled for a few seconds.

"Is Finn coming with us?" Mrs Mace laughed.

"Can he?" Jack asked, his heart skipping a beat before he quickly realised his teacher was joking.

For a few seconds neither Mrs Mace nor Mum said anything. Jack knew they were doing that thing where two adults look at each other and silently pass a message between them.

"Here." Mrs Mace handed Jack a plastic wallet. "Your file. There's information about the D-Day trip. A diary for you to fill in each night while we are away. And your cross."

Three of Jack's classmates came past, each carrying a pillow and a cuddly toy. At first Jack wanted to laugh. Cuddly toy? How soft were they? Then he saw one of the cuddly toys was a dog and he felt his throat tighten and the space behind his eyes go all hot.

"This way, please," Jack heard 6B's class teacher, Mr Thompson, say. "First-class and business travellers upstairs, please."

Jack jumped as he heard some adults laugh loudly at Mr Thompson's joke, and he looked round quickly. That was when the cross dropped out of his plastic folder. Finn saw it fall, but the dog's attention was too fixed on Jack to want to pick it up.

"I'll look after Finn," Mum was saying. "You know I will. I'll send you photos of him every day. You need to be strong, Jack. Just say goodbye to him now. He'll be fine. You will be too. I know you."

Jack's mum's words cut through his feelings. She was right. And, anyway, he had no choice with everyone watching him.

Jack squatted. "Finn? Look at me."

Finn stared deep into Jack's eyes.

"I'll be back. Just a few days. Then I'll be back. Understand?"

Finn's eyes stayed fixed on Jack's. *He's asking me why I'm going*, Jack thought. Jack stared back into his dog's eyes and tried to reassure him, thinking about all the things they'd do when he got home. Thinking too about Glen and Emile Corteil and how they could communicate like this: reading each other's minds, speaking without words.

I'm coming back, Jack said without speaking.

Jack felt pretty sure Finn would get the message.

Jack breathed in deeply, grabbed Finn's collar and growled into his dog's furry neck. Then he stood up and felt his mum kiss his head. Jack was sure that some of the others were watching him, wondering whether he was going to back out.

"Go," she said.

So Jack went. Up the steps to the top deck. Not looking back. The first time away from home, from Finn, from his mum. And Dad.

Upstairs there were sixty-six seats in twos running the length of the bus, with an aisle in between. Strip lights along the ceiling illuminated his classmates' grinning faces. Because it was dark, the windows of the bus acted like mirrors, making it look like there were over a hundred children, not sixty. Bags of sweets were being handed round.

"Jack? With me!" Lucas had saved a place for him.

Jack sat next to his friend.

"Look," Lucas said, "I can see your mum. And Finn. But your dad's not there ..."

Jack stared down and saw his mum among the other parents, waving. Finn looked anxious, like he was desperate to find Jack. Then he started to howl his don't-leave-me howl. Even though he knew Finn would be fine at home with Mum, Jack still felt bad. Really bad.

Jack noticed the driver stoop to pick something up off the floor by the coach door before he climbed into the driver's seat. He'd probably dropped his cigarettes.

The engine was on now, the bus quivering, like Finn at the door before a walk.

When the bus moved out of the school car park

onto the main road, Jack craned his neck to get a last glimpse, past Lucas, of Finn. When all he could see was darkness, he sat back and wiped his eyes with his sleeve.

Kasandra was sitting across the aisle. She was the only one who noticed that Jack was upset.

"Are you OK?" she asked in a quiet voice.

Jack shrugged. "Just about." He tried to smile.

"He is a nice dog. What is his name?"

"Finn."

"Finn? I like that. I think your dog was looking for you."

Jack felt his eyes well up with hot tears. He nodded, failed to smile for a second time and looked out of the window.

SIXTEEN

For the first hour of the journey south to Portsmouth ferry port, 6A and 6B chatted excitedly, passing sweets and crisps around, pointing at the sides of lorries and other coaches on unlit motorways. Then gradually it became quieter, and two hours into the journey, Jack was pretty sure he was the only one still awake. He looked around the interior of the coach. Black windows. Dark seat covers. Paper and plastic wrappers in the aisle between him and Kasandra.

Jack liked the quiet when everyone else was asleep. He had a lot to think about.

Home. What would be happening now?

Would Mum and Dad be at the kitchen table sorting things out? That's what Dad had said they'd do. They'd talk. Over endless cups of tea. And if they were still awake, would Finn be awake? He might be on his mat under the kitchen table. Would he be waiting for Jack to come home? Or would he be thinking about his next bowl of food?

Jack smiled. He hoped his dog would be thinking about food.

Jack stared out of the coach window and wondered if dogs thought things over like people did. As he saw the world flashing by, he couldn't help his thoughts turning – again – to Corteil and Glen. What if Finn was on this coach and Jack just threw him out of the window? That would be the same thing. Jack just couldn't stop torturing himself with these terrible thoughts. He seemed to have no control over them, however upsetting they were.

He tried to focus on the headlights of cars and trucks coming the other way on the motorway, trying to get his body comfortable, leaning his head against the window, then the seat in front of him as the bus carried on its journey south.

Then he must have fallen asleep.

SEVENTEEN

Jack woke up when the bus stuttered to a halt. He'd been half thinking or dreaming about his dad, wondering if, when he got home, his dad would have moved back in and everything would be back to normal again.

Fully awake, he looked around and studied everyone in the darkness. Ghostly reflections of sleeping children's faces, some pressing pillows against windows. Jack had insisted to his mum that he didn't need a pillow. He'd look stupid with a pillow, he said. Now he felt stupid for *not* having one. Everyone else had a pillow. Everyone else was asleep.

The bus, he realised, had stopped. Jack wondered if they were in Portsmouth for the ferry already. But he knew they weren't supposed to arrive on the south coast of England until six or seven and it would be light by then.

Jack heard the door hydraulics hiss and watched the driver exit and walk the length of the bus to light a cigarette, exhaling a plume of smoke and staring upwards into the night sky as if he was searching for something up there. Jack narrowed his eyes and studied the driver. What was it about him that bothered Jack so much?

Jack put his hand out to stroke Finn. He stopped himself before he put his hand on Lucas's knee, then heard a soft laugh and glanced across the aisle at Kasandra. The Syrian girl smiled at him.

"Do you miss him?" she asked.

Jack nodded. He knew she was talking about Finn.

"He'll be in his crate now," Jack explained. "He sleeps in the kitchen in a crate. It sounds bad. It sounds like he's in a cage. But he likes it. He has his toys in it."

"My dogs used to sleep in a crate too. It's good."

Jack was pleased Kasandra had said something to him about her life again. He wanted to ask where her dogs were now. But he wasn't sure if he should. Would they have travelled here with her? Probably not. Had she come over the sea from Syria, in one of those tiny rubber boats with too many people in? They would never have dogs in those too. Jack had heard it cost thousands for a person to go in one of the boats. Would people bring dogs too?

Boats. Jack looked at Kasandra. She was staring straight ahead now. *What if she's scared of boats?* She might be.

"Kasandra?"

"Yes?"

"You can hang around with me and Lucas on the ferry from Portsmouth to France if you want. There'll be lots of fun things to do. There's a cinema, I think. Shops. A cafe. We could have a really good time."

Kasandra's face lit up. "Yes. Yes, please," she said. "That would be nice."

EIGHTEEN

Jack had never been abroad before, so when the coach rolled off the ferry the next afternoon he sat up tall to see what another country might look like.

Everything that caught his eye looked weird. French words on the sides of trucks. Funny number plates on cars. Long lines of tall trees on either side of some of the roads. Then the buildings: they were all boxy and some of them looked like they were made of wood, not stone.

Jack saw a lady walking two spaniels that looked a bit like Finn. He leaned over Lucas to see them properly.

Lucas shook his head. "Don't go near French dogs," his friend said. "They have rabies, and when they bite you, you get rabies too and you die of thirst, frothing at the mouth, and it's the worst way of dying."

"Nice," Jack said. "I'll watch out."

Jack looked over the aisle at Kasandra. She grinned at him. They'd had a good time together on the ferry. The three of them. Jack had tried to keep Kasandra busy in case being on the water was bringing back bad memories for her.

The coach drove on. And Jack felt good. He liked being on a coach with his friends from school. Danny and Kofi were in the seats behind them, being funny. Yes, he missed Finn. But this was nice too.

The thing that threw Jack most about France was the roundabouts, because everyone was driving on the wrong side of the road, meaning the coach went round them the wrong way too. Even though

Jack had known this was going to happen, he grabbed on to the side of his seat in astonishment. For a second he felt like the bus would roll over.

But it didn't. Of course.

Out of the ferry port, the coach accelerated onto a three-lane motorway heading towards the area where Jack and his schoolmates were going to spend the next few days visiting places where hundreds of men were killed fighting in the Second World War.

Jack sighed and remembered why he didn't want to be here.

So why *was* he here?

It was a simple question with a simple answer: he was in France so that he wasn't in England, meaning Mum and Dad could talk and Dad could make a decision about Afghanistan.

Jack shook his head. He was here so he wasn't there. He was apart from his family so they could be together. He was surrounded by people when he wanted to be alone. He was here to celebrate war even though he hated war.

It was crazy.

Now there was another question in his head. It was about the thought he'd just had.

Did he hate war?

Was that true?

Not so long ago he had revelled in playing violent video games with his dad. He had been thrilled that his dad was about to go to fight in a war himself. Proud of him. He had loved soldiers and soldiering and war. But now? Now Jack thought that war was madness. Now he hated soldiers. Especially ones who put dogs in danger. Like Emile Corteil.

Jack swallowed back a surge of sadness. He decided to count the time gaps between the road signs. That would stop him thinking.

NINETEEN

An hour or so after getting off the ferry, they made a stop at a museum where they watched a 360-degree surround film about D-Day, then they moved on to the place that was to be their home for the next three days.

The film they had watched in the museum had been exciting, but worrying too. It had shown wave after wave falling on the beach. But not waves of water – waves of men.

Being shot.

Being shelled.

Being killed.

Then there were images of the sea itself: not frothy and sparkling like the sea should be. But red. A sea of blood. It had overwhelmed Jack because you had to keep looking around you, behind you and back again to understand the film in all 360 degrees. By the end he was dizzy. And sickened by war.

At the end of the film the narrator had said:

They gave their tomorrow so we could
have our today.

As they had driven away from the museum, Jack had been trying to work out what that meant.

Here *he* was today where all those men had given *their* tomorrows.

Jack had shaken his head.

They were stupid, then. All of them.

He'd gone into the museum to try to make a

good start to the school trip. But it had only made him feel worse. He'd stay on the bus next time.

The residential building where Jack and his classmates would be staying was a very large stone-built house. It had fifteen bedrooms on four floors, a dining hall and there were other rooms behind closed doors that Mr Thompson said the children were not to enter. The floors were tiled, with no carpets, so every voice and footstep echoed round the corridor as the children – having unloaded their bags with Miss Khan – raced to their rooms.

Outside, the stone walls were hidden by the green leaves and dangling purple flowers of an enormous climbing plant. Its roots twined and twisted round the window frames and up onto the slate roof. A soft breeze wafted a sweet fragrance in through the open windows.

In front of the house there was a gravel

driveway with a turning circle. To the left, a huge field with an orchard at the far end.

With an hour to go before dinner, Jack received a text from his mum. A selfie of her and Finn by the river at home. It was good to see Finn but Jack was unsettled by the fact there was no sign of Dad in the photo. A selfie meant there was no one else there to take a better photo of the two of them. Meaning no Dad. They were not together. And that was not good.

Jack asked if he could go for a short walk on his own, to stretch his legs and write his diary in the fields beyond the house. Given permission, he headed for the long grass at the edge of the orchard. He went there because Finn liked nosing his way through long grass. He smiled to himself. He was going to places his dog would like, even though his dog was hundreds of miles away. That was a bit crazy.

"You miss him," he said to himself.

As he spoke, he saw someone sitting in the dry grass. Kasandra, staring up at the branches of a tree. She had her diary on her knee, a pen poised over it, as if she was thinking what to write.

"Who are you talking to?" she said.

Jack scratched his head. "Me."

"Just you?"

Jack grinned and blushed. "Yeah."

"Maybe you were pretending your dog is here."

"I sort of was," Jack said. She was right, after all.

"You miss him still?"

"Yes."

"My dogs were called Loki and Lucy," Kasandra said. "Lucy is dead. And Loki is probably dead. I don't know."

Jack felt his throat tighten. Kasandra was

opening up about her life again. He didn't want to make her feel sad by asking her more about it, but he didn't want to ignore what she'd said either.

"Is Loki in Syria?" he tried.

"Yes. When we left Aleppo – my city – we could not take him. He ran away and we did not know where he was."

Jack looked at Kasandra but didn't speak.

"But Aleppo is not a good place to live," Kasandra said. "There were bombs and not much food. Soldiers. Loki was frightened."

"Of the soldiers?"

"And the bombs."

Jack desperately wanted to say something nice to Kasandra, something to try to make her feel better.

"Maybe he found some other dogs," he suggested, "and they formed a pack and they went out into the countryside together and are there now?"

Kasandra smiled broadly. "I hope so. That is a nice idea. I don't like it when people are bad to dogs. It upsets me."

The two of them sat in silence. Warm air moved slowly through the trees around them. A pair of white butterflies danced above their heads.

Jack wanted to ask Kasandra about her home. But he wasn't sure how to, without sounding rude. But then Kasandra spoke again, as if she'd read his thoughts.

"Some of our house fell down," she said.

Jack frowned. "Why? What happened? Was it old?"

"No. It was new. It was hit by a bomb when I was in school and my parents were at work. Lucy was in the garden. She was killed. We found her body under a collapsed wall. That was when Loki ran away."

"I ..."

"So the next day we left Aleppo. We took only the bags we could carry. That's all. Everything else we left behind."

Jack suddenly felt a hot rush of emotions.

"I didn't know," Jack said.

"I have not told anyone. How would you know?"

"I mean I'm sorry for what I said in school before we left home. About people who get caught in war. I didn't know about what happened to you."

Kasandra smiled. "It's OK."

Jack was staring back at the house. He could see Mr Salah and Mrs Mace watching him and Kasandra from the doorway.

"It is OK now," Kasandra repeated. "But please don't tell the others about it. I like it that I have just told you. But I don't want to talk about it to anyone else."

"Deal," Jack said. "I promise."

TWENTY

Day two in France. The coach moved slowly down the hill towards the coastline. Jack could hear shouts and laughter as Kofi pointed out the sandy beach and sunlight sparkled on the waves. Jack peered out of the window with Lucas. Lucas was bouncing up and down in his seat with excitement.

The children filed off the bus and gathered in a large circle on a grass bank behind the coach park. Mr Salah stood on a low wall to address them. Behind them was a long wide beach that disappeared into a shimmering haze down the coast, a vast blue sky and flat silvery sea behind it. The day was becoming hotter and hotter, the cool of early morning evaporating.

"Do you remember how we learned in the museum yesterday that thousands of men died here on Omaha Beach?" Mr Salah said in a calm but clear voice. "They came from the sea, taking their first steps to put an end to the Nazi domination of Europe. They were prepared to risk their lives to try to drive the Nazis back into Germany, to save the millions of people who were dying and suffering under German rule in Europe."

"The sea was red," Lucas whispered.

"What?" Jack asked. It was hard to focus on what Lucas was saying; he felt so uneasy about the beach and the terrible things that had happened here.

"With blood," Lucas added.

"I know," Jack muttered, noticing that Miss Khan was watching Lucas very carefully.

"They were shot at, shelled and had flame-throwers turned on them," Mr Salah went on. "Thousands died. They gave their lives so that we can come here to enjoy the freedom of the land and sand and sea. We are free to do this because they died right here. Remember what we heard at the museum yesterday: *They gave their tomorrow so we could have our today*. Think about that."

Silence. None of Year 6 knew quite what to do next. Or say. They just stood with their arms limp at their sides. Thinking. Jack remembered the line about the soldiers giving their tomorrows. He looked out at the beach where they had died, and frowned.

Then Mrs Mace appeared with a large blue sports bag.

"Yesterday," she said, "was very intense. We had a long journey and then – even before we reached our accommodation – we visited a museum and saw a very emotional film. We think it is time you all had some fun. And after what we have heard from Mr Salah, I can't think of anything better for children to do on this beach than play, enjoying your freedom, your today."

And so Year 6 played on the beach where thousands of men had lost their lives. Mrs Mace had made that feel like it was the most fitting thing they could do. They threw themselves into it. Mrs Mace and Miss Khan watched the game from the touchline, chatting as they lifted their faces to the sun.

Jack and Lucas joined in a game of football. A pitch was drawn out on the sand, just next to some sand dunes where Mr Thompson and Mr Salah were sitting. Large sticks for goalposts, with a pile of stones to hold them straight.

Jack felt good, throwing himself into the game, tackling, leaping into the air, laughing as he fell with Kasandra and Ella and Kofi on the beach. The sand was soft, so every tackle and lunge at the ball became more and more exaggerated. Jack was laughing so hard he could barely run or look up to see who was in his team.

It felt good. Really good.

Until Lucas saw a dog running towards them through the waves.

TWENTY-ONE

"There's a dog! There's a dog!" Lucas was shouting so loudly that all the children had stopped where they were and stood looking at him.

It was a large dog – a wolfhound, something like that – barking loudly as it ran at speed through the waves that were hitting the beach. Even though Jack could see the dog was playing and wasn't a threat to any of them, he recognised panic in Lucas's voice and remembered his friend telling him that French dogs had rabies and could kill you with a single bite.

Jack jogged over to Lucas. He could solve this.

"Lucas, come with me."

"No," Lucas said, then he was shouting again, bending to pick something off the beach. "There's a dog!"

That was when the dog looked over and slowed down. Jack could see something in its eyes. It was interested. Jack knew that dogs liked excitement, that they were drawn to people calling out and picking things up off the floor. Which was exactly what Lucas was doing now, grabbing stones from the goalpost, ready to defend himself.

So now the dog was coming, veering towards them. Inquisitive. Whatever sort of game this small boy was going to play, the dog wanted to join in. And as the dog raced towards them, Lucas began to throw stone after stone at it.

That was when Jack heard Kasandra scream. "Stop! Don't hurt the dog!"

Jack looked across at her and remembered

another conversation from the previous day. Kasandra had been so upset about her own dog being hurt and Jack desperately wanted to stop her feeling bad again. So he lunged at Lucas, pushing him to the floor. Then he grabbed one of the sticks they'd been using as a goalpost and stood over his friend, drawing it back.

"Stop it!" Jack yelled at Lucas, standing frozen in his attack position.

Jack never intended to hit Lucas. He just wanted to scare him to make him stop throwing stones at the dog.

An arm came around Jack and snatched the stick from his hand. Jack turned and looked into a pair of angry eyes.

Mr Salah.

Then Jack looked back down at Lucas and saw how he was lying on his side, arms over his head, legs pulled up to his stomach, his mouth wide open and a terrible scream coming out of it.

The rest of the class were led quickly to the bus by Mrs Mace and Mr Thompson. Lucas was with Miss Khan. But Mr Salah kept Jack back, away from the others. Jack noticed that the driver was watching them, smoking a cigarette, leaning against the side of his bus.

"I know things are difficult at home, Jack," Mr Salah said. "I know that, and I've been really pleased – so far – with how you were coping with the trip. But this? Why would you do that? I just don't understand."

Jack shrugged.

"I need to know why, Jack. This is serious. You pushed him over. If you'd hit Lucas with that stick, you could ... well, I don't know what."

Jack knew what this was. It was Mr Salah giving

him the chance to explain what he'd done. Mr Salah was always fair. And if Jack told him that Kasandra had opened up about her life in Syria and that she was still upset about her dogs, Mr Salah might understand. Jack might even avoid punishment. But Kasandra had been very clear: Jack was not to tell anyone else about their conversation.

"Jack," Mr Salah said, his voice less patient now. "Why did you do it?"

"There was a reason," Jack said.

"What is it, then?" Mr Salah frowned. "Was it to do with this beach? I mean, Jack, this is where men fought and died so we would all be free, so we wouldn't have to fight. Do you understand how your behaviour might have upset people here?"

Jack stared out to sea. "I do," he replied.

"So why?" Mr Salah pressed.

Jack didn't answer. He just stared at the sea,

squinting into the light. The waves were breaking in lines on the beach. Jack tried to imagine soldiers coming through the waves, falling one after the other, the sea a great tide of bodies.

"One last time, Jack. Why did you do it? I have to know how to respond to this and you can help me. But if you can't give me a good answer, then there will have to be repercussions."

"I can't say," Jack shrugged.

TWENTY-TWO

The road was wide and long. Jack could see everything through the massive front window of the coach, yellow-brown crop fields stretching out ahead of him on either side of a long winding strip of tarmac.

Above him the coach was quieter than usual. Because of what he'd done. At the beach.

Jack was sitting at the front of the coach with the driver. Mr Salah had made Jack apologise to Lucas, but Lucas had not even looked him in the eye or replied. Isolation was Jack's punishment. Being away from the other children.

The driver had four things on a shelf between

their two large upright seats. A takeaway coffee cup. A packet of cigarettes. A large bag of Jelly Babies. And a thick paperback book with the words "Merville Battery" on it. The book reminded Jack of something he'd read about D-Day. He couldn't quite remember what. But the Jelly Babies had his attention. He was hoping the driver might share them with him. But he wasn't going to ask.

Jack stared at the road. He was thirsty. He put his hand to his throat.

"You feel sick?" the driver asked quickly.

Jack shook his head and looked at the man. He smelled of smoke. He had blurry tattoos on his arms. And Jack couldn't see his eyes because he was wearing sunglasses.

The driver raised his sunglasses and studied Jack. "Well, if you do feel sick, don't do it in my coach. Got it?"

Jack scowled and turned his head to study the road again. They were on a two-lane road now, leading to a roundabout.

After more silence, the driver asked Jack, "See that man in the uniform?"

Jack shook his head.

"Well, look up, then."

"I don't want to," Jack muttered.

"You don't want to?" The man's voice was harsh.

"No."

The driver stopped talking and began to steer the bus round a large roundabout.

"There's a statue in the middle of this roundabout," the driver said. "A man in a uniform. His name is Eisenhower. He's important. Just look at him."

Because the driver's voice was softer now, Jack looked up and saw the statue of a man in a uniform at the centre of the roundabout, hands on his hips, staring down the road. Behind the statue there was an arch. Jack watched the driver control the bus so that it eased off the roundabout and onto another road.

"The course of history depends on your success," the driver said in an American accent.

Jack didn't reply. But he could feel the driver looking at him.

"Do you know what Eisenhower meant by that?" the driver asked.

Jack heard laughter from upstairs. He wondered if some of the other Year 6s were laughing at him, stuck up front with the chain-smoking nonsense-speaking driver.

"Do you know what it means?" the driver said again.

Jack felt a flash of anger. "I don't care," he snapped.

The driver laughed. But it was a dark laugh. Not

a we're-having-a-nice-time-at-the-front-of-the-bus sort of laugh.

"You don't care what Dwight Eisenhower said to the thousands of soldiers who came here and struggled up the beaches or parachuted in pitch darkness before getting their heads blown off?"

Jack felt cold even though the sun was belting through the windows. He moved his feet, knocking the driver's book.

"Sorry," he muttered quietly.

He looked at the driver's arms. They were muscular, especially when he turned the steering wheel. They were like thick pieces of rope Jack had seen at a harbour at the seaside. A series of plaited knots. That's what it reminded Jack of, anyway.

And Jack wondered just how long he was going to have to sit with the driver. He didn't know if he could bear it.

TWENTY-THREE

For the next twenty minutes the driver said nothing to Jack as he guided the large double-decker coach through country lanes and between tight fields bordered with hedgerows that Jack could not see through.

"So, talk to me. What's your problem?" the driver finally asked.

Jack wasn't going to reply, but he was bored and he wanted another argument with the driver. He quite liked it that the driver was letting him be cross, even rude. He never normally got to talk to adults like this.

"What?" Jack asked, trying to sound like he wasn't interested in what the driver was saying.

"What do you mean you don't care? You don't care about learning about the war?"

"It's stupid. That's all," Jack said.

"What's stupid?" the driver asked.

"War," Jack answered.

"Is it?"

"Yes."

"Every war? Every soldier?"

"Yes."

"Have you always been a pacifist?" the driver asked.

"A what?"

"Pacifist. Someone who is against war."

"No," Jack muttered.

"So, what brought it on?"

Jack turned to the driver. "I found stuff out."

“What stuff?”

“Stuff about war. D-Day. And Syria. It’s stupid.”

“Go on,” the driver said.

Jack paused. He thought about Corteil throwing Glen out of the plane and gritted his teeth, feeling angry again. Why did people want to make him stop thinking that war was stupid? Why were they always trying to make him feel like he was wrong?

“They used animals,” Jack snapped. “Dogs. Horses. Even pigeons. People can choose to go and fight in a war. But dogs don’t get to choose if they’re thrown out of planes by people, do they?”

“But the animals helped,” the driver insisted. “Without them we might not have won the war.”

“The animals died. Most of them.”

“So did the men,” the driver said.

“I don’t care about the men,” Jack said. “They could choose to go. But Glen didn’t. He didn’t want to jump. He was cowering under a bench. Emile Corteil threw him out of the plane anyway. That's not fair. Corteil can die if he wants to. But why should Glen?"

"Glen?" The driver was smiling. "Tell me about Glen and Emile."

"And what about children being killed in war?" Jack carried on with his rant. "What about Syria? Is that all right?"

The driver dropped the coach down a gear and Jack watched his arms power the wheel round as the bus took a steep left turn uphill.

"Well, Syria. That's different, but—"

"But D-Day was OK? The Second World War was OK? Millions of people died. Most of them were bombed or gassed or stuff like that."

"I know that."

"But you still think it's good?"

"No, I think it's terrible." The driver raised his

voice. "Of course it's terrible. It's the worst of things. But can I ask *you* a question?"

The bus was slowing down as the driver took a left now, into a huge car park surrounded by squared-off hedges and grass banks that looked like they had been mown that morning. They parked alongside at least twenty other coaches.

"Can I?" the driver asked again.

"If you want."

"This place here. This is where we are visiting next. It's the American Cemetery. There are thousands of men buried on the hill. How do you think it feels to come out of the sea, thousands of miles from your family, from your home, knowing there's a damn good chance you're going to be shot in the face or chest before you're out of the water, or shelled on your way up the beach as you try to get through the barbed wire? Do you think soldiers like that?"

"They must do," Jack said. "They do it, don't they?"

"It's not as simple as that," the driver said, pulling his handbrake hard.

"What's not simple?"

"The reasons you do it."

Jack laughed at the driver. "How would you know anyway?" he asked scornfully.

The driver hesitated. "I know," he said, then slipped out of his seat, pushed his door open and stalked to the back of the bus to light a cigarette.

Jack was left wondering what the driver had meant. I *know*, he'd said, in a way that sounded like he did know. Was it just because the man read books about war, like the one on his dashboard? Or was Jack missing something?

TWENTY-FOUR

Mr Salah emerged from behind the driver's seat and asked Jack to join the others on the top deck. Jack followed. Though he had already made his mind up about the American Cemetery.

"As you know," Mr Salah began, "we're about to visit the Normandy American Cemetery. This is where nearly 9,400 US soldiers are buried. Most of them died on Omaha Beach, where we played earlier."

Silence.

"Some rules about this cemetery," Mr Salah advised. "The Americans expect visitors to keep to the paths and to remain very quiet at all times. No calling out. No wandering among the graves."

Mr Salah paused as Mrs Mace and Mr Thompson appeared at the front of the coach behind him.

"Part of the reason for this," he went on, "is that you will see some very old men here who are also visiting. In their nineties. They may well be former American soldiers returning here to remember their part in the D-Day assault, where they will have lost friends in the bloodshed. They may well have been among those who landed on Omaha Beach."

Jack kept his eyes closed as the rest of Year 6 got off the bus. He was imagining what he would say if he met one of the men in their nineties.

Idiot? Would he say that?

No. Of course he wouldn't, but it would be what he was thinking. Men – and they always seemed to be men – were idiots for shooting and bombing and causing people like Kasandra to suffer and dogs like Glen to die. Men like Dad who thought it was funny to want to go to another country and kill people – and play video games about it with their sons. Jack didn't want to walk around a stupid cemetery pretending to feel sad about those men.

Jack watched Lucas join Kasandra to walk to the cemetery. He tried to catch his friend's eye, but Lucas was looking only at Miss Khan.

"Jack?" It was Mrs Mace. "Come on, Jack," she said.

Jack shook his head. "I'm not coming," he said.

TWENTY-FIVE

Once Jack's classmates had come back from the American Cemetery and were on board, the coach driver began reversing out of his parking bay, waving to one of the other drivers and steering the bus towards the exit.

Jack sat staring at his lap, still exiled up front with the driver. He'd tried again to catch Lucas's eye as Year 6 walked back from the cemetery, but Lucas wouldn't look at him. Jack felt alone. He missed Finn, his mum, his dad. And now his friend.

Once they were on the road, Jack looked across at the driver.

"What did you mean?" he asked.

"Eh?" The driver looked confused.

"When you said *I know*?" Jack said. "What did you mean?"

The driver pressed his foot on the accelerator as they climbed a hill. "I know about war," he said. "That's all."

"What do you know?"

"I was in the army for twenty-two years. We dropped into the Falkland Islands. 1982."

"Parachuted?"

"Yeah."

"You?"

"Yes. Me. Don't look so surprised."

"But why?" Jack asked.

"Why what?"

"Why did you parachute into the … Where did you say?"

"The Falkland Islands?" The driver sat up straight and checked his mirror before moving out into the fast lane. "Well, in a nutshell, Argentina invaded the Falkland Islands in 1982. And the people who live there wanted to be British, not Argie. So Maggie Thatcher – that was our prime minister then – sent a task force of ships and planes all the way to the Falklands to sort them out. Which we did."

"How far are the Falkland Islands?" Jack asked.

"Eight thousand miles."

"And you were with them?"

"I was."

The driver tapped the indicator and made a left at a roundabout. Neither he nor Jack spoke for a minute. Jack couldn't believe what he was hearing. This old man had once been a young paratrooper. Like Corteil. Like all those others.

"What was it like?" Jack asked.

"It was all right."

"But ... what was it like jumping out of a plane into a war?"

The driver laughed. "Well ... it felt like jumping out of a plane into a war."

Jack hesitated. It was a stupid answer. How did the driver expect him to understand if he just said things like that? He tried again.

"But what did it *feel* like?"

"I said."

"But why? Why did you do it?" Jack asked.

The driver stared hard at the road ahead. "You might find out when we visit the Pegasus Bridge Museum tomorrow."

Jack wanted to know what the driver meant, but he decided not to push it. He found it hard to believe that he was sitting next to a paratrooper. Like the men who'd dropped into Normandy to liberate France. What did you say to someone who'd done something like that?

TWENTY-SIX

Back at the house that evening, the children were exhausted. Jack went to sit with the teachers at dinner time. But before the food was served, Jack realised that Lucas was standing behind him.

"You're allowed to come and sit with me now," Lucas said, turning to leave.

Jack stood up, followed Lucas and sat at a small table with him and Kasandra.

"Hi," Jack said to Kasandra. Then he looked at Lucas until Lucas returned Jack's gaze.

"I'm sorry about the beach," Jack said. "I'm so sorry."

"It's OK now," Lucas said cheerfully. "Kassie's told me that there was a reason you did it and you were doing it to be nice to her, so I don't mind, because Kassie is my friend. If you were being nice to her, then it's OK."

Jack looked at Kasandra. "Thanks," he mouthed.

Kasandra smiled back.

The three of them ate in silence. Jack listened in to the conversations of some of his classmates above the clatter of crockery and cutlery, a couple of chairs falling over, the shouts of teachers asking for everyone to be quiet. But no one was talking about the American Cemetery. Jack sort of wished they were. After what the coach driver had said to him, he was keen to know what it was like. Although he didn't want to admit it.

After a meal of a thick tomato soup with crusty bread, followed by a dark and sugary custard pudding, the children dispersed to write their diaries or play in the grounds of the house and the games room. Lucas went to write his diary with Miss Khan.

Jack couldn't see Kasandra. He wondered if she was back underneath the apple tree at the far side of the orchard. Taking his diary, he walked out of the house, then across the lawn, through the warm evening sunlight.

He found her there. She was writing in her own diary.

"You like it here," he said.

Kasandra smiled. "It is peaceful."

They sat together for a moment. Kasandra didn't mention what had happened on the beach. Jack didn't want to raise it unless she did. But he did want to talk about Lucas.

"I came to say thank you for talking to Lucas."

"It is OK," Kasandra said. "You were trying

to protect my feelings." The Syrian girl hesitated. "Weren't you?"

"I was." Jack coughed, then, changing the subject, asked, "Er ... so ... what was it like today?"

"In the American Cemetery?"

"Yeah."

"It was sad. There are thousands of white crosses for Christians. And some stars and domes for Jewish and Muslim men. So many. Each for a man who died."

"How did you feel?"

Kasandra's face clouded over. "Different things. Sad. Proud. Envious."

"Envious?" Jack asked. He couldn't imagine what she meant.

"Yes."

"Of who? The soldiers?"

"No. Not them. Sad for the soldiers. Proud of

the soldiers. What I was envious of was the French people. They still live here because an army invaded from the sea."

"Oh ..." Jack suddenly understood what Kasandra meant. No army had come from the sea to liberate Syria. "I wish someone had come to help you," he said.

"I pretend they did. Or they will. And that we can go home."

Jack nodded. He watched two ducks fly low over the tops of the trees in the orchard. The sun was going down, the sky changing from its bright blue to a deeper shade. The orchard was partly in shadow now.

"I wish you had come to the cemetery today," Kasandra said suddenly.

Jack didn't reply.

"And I think you will be sad if you don't go to Emile Corteil's grave tomorrow," she added.

Jack breathed, then sighed. He didn't want to think about Emile Corteil.

"I read about what happened," Kasandra said. "To him. And to Glen."

Jack swallowed. "Then you know why I don't want to go to his grave," he told her.

TWENTY-SEVEN

Day three, after breakfast. Mr Salah offered Jack the chance to sit with Lucas and Kasandra on the journey to Pegasus Bridge. But the driver – who had been standing near Jack since he'd come out of the house, smoking two or three cigarettes one after the other – overheard.

"Not possible, sir," the driver intervened, coughing. "I'm not done with this one yet."

Mr Salah shrugged and made Jack sit up front again. Deep down, Jack was quite pleased.

"You asked me why I did it?" the driver said, turning to Jack once they were on the road.

"Yes." Jack leaned forward in his chair.

"If I tell you, will you do something for me in return?"

"OK."

"You promise?"

"I do." Jack was desperate to know now. Why did soldiers do what they did? Maybe if he understood the driver's actions, he would be able to understand what Corteil had done. And then he might understand his dad more clearly too.

"It was thrilling," the driver started. "The best buzz ever. It was what I had trained for all my adult life. To fight in a war for my country. I was being who I wanted to be. But also ..."

"Yeah?"

"Well, also, it was the most frightening day of my life. As I dropped into the cold and wet and dark, I expected a bullet to hit me. And when I landed, I expected a bayonet to be thrust at me, or to step on a mine – to suffer some form of slow, painful death. And it terrified me. And, yes, actually I did feel like an idiot."

"So why did you do it?" Jack asked.

"Because I was fighting for my country. And, even more, for the men either side of me on the plane."

"Even though you were scared?"

"Even more so," the driver said. "Sometimes that makes it easier. If you're scared, you know it's important."

Jack nodded. Neither of them spoke for a minute. The coach drew up outside a small glass-fronted building with a large metal structure behind it. Jack was surprised. He'd not noticed where they had driven; he'd been so involved in the conversation with the coach driver.

They had arrived at the Pegasus Bridge Museum. It was time to get off.

"So, now you have to do something for me." The driver clapped Jack gently on the back.

"What?"

"This museum is about a group of men who dropped down onto this strip of land by the canal in gliders." The driver pointed at a canal. "They had to capture a bridge and hold it, so the German army couldn't come over it and attack the Allies as they made their beach landings. The men in the gliders knew they had a good chance of being killed. But they still did it. They wanted to stop Hitler and to do the right thing because they could. Even if it cost them their lives."

Jack noticed a wobble in the driver's voice. He said nothing.

"I want you to go round this museum," the

driver continued, “and I want you to think about what you hear and see. Then I want you to come out and tell me if you think those men, Emile Corteil, and me for that matter, are idiots. I want you to make your own mind up. Deal?”

Jack frowned. He didn’t have much choice. He’d made a promise.

“Deal,” he said.

TWENTY-EIGHT

The museum was small and dwarfed by the massive grey bridge in the clearing behind it; next to that stood a large wooden glider about the same size as the coach they had been travelling in, but with wings.

On one side of the museum there was a canal. On the other side, a river. Inside, display panels and objects in glass cases told the story of the brave British soldiers who had landed on this narrow strip to stop the Germans transporting troops to the beaches to attack the Allies. At the centre there was a huge 3D model of the area, showing the Merville Battery, Pegasus Bridge, Ranville. The children gathered round it, pressing buttons to illuminate different places on the battlefield.

Photographs were projected onto a screen around the 3D map and Jack looked at the faces of these men who felt like real people to him now. Courageous soldiers doing what they thought they should do, like the coach driver had told him. Their faces were determined, all fixed jaws and fiery stares. Determined to defeat Hitler and the Nazis, to stop what they were doing to Europe and the world.

Jack knew that they were not idiots or stupid. Quite the opposite.

He felt confused. Confused about how he wanted to feel. Then he remembered something Mr Salah had said earlier in the trip: *They were prepared to risk their lives to try to drive the Nazis back into Germany, to save the millions of people who were dying and suffering under German rule in Europe.*

He could see that sense of purpose in the faces on the screens. He could see fear too. Jack felt a chill run up his spine.

Was this what Emile Corteil would have looked like that night he'd jumped with Glen? So determined to defeat Hitler, knowing he needed Glen with him?

And what about Jack's own dad? What was his reason for wanting to be a soldier? To feel like that? To do something good? Not something bad. Wasn't that what Jack's dad had learned watching war films with his own dad?

Now Jack got it. He understood.

These were young men – like the coach driver had been years before with his friends – putting their lives at risk, not because they liked war and wanted to kill, but because they thought they were doing the right thing.

To stop Hitler. To change the course of history.

Jack felt tears on his cheeks. He was crying. And Jack hated crying. Especially in front of other children. He wanted his dad. Right now. Right here. And Finn. He wanted Finn.

He stumbled into a corner, coming right up against a display board showing more pictures of paratroopers, dozens of young men who had dropped into this exact place to do what they thought was right.

Jack focused his eyes only to see he was looking at a photograph. He stepped back, shocked. It was like it was meant to be.

He wiped his sleeve across his face and stared hard at the photograph – a young man wearing a paratrooper's beret and uniform. He was staring back at Jack, his legs apart, with a look of fierce determination on his face. Next to him, a German Shepherd dog, ears back.

Emile Corteil and Glen.

Jack stood and stared. He wasn't sure for how long. He was trying to piece together the details of what had happened to Glen and Corteil. To tell himself the story again. He felt himself shiver. He heard a voice. Lucas calling his name.

"I'm here." Jack turned to call back and saw Lucas and Kasandra coming round a corner.

"There he is. Jack? Are you OK?" asked Lucas.

"I'm fine. I was just looking at this. Come and see. I want to show you."

Lucas came to stand right next to Jack, their shoulders touching. Kasandra stood behind them, looking between their heads.

"You found them," she said. "This is Emile and Glen. Yes?"

Jack felt the shiver pass along his arms. He looked down to see the hairs on his arms were raised.

"Yes," he said. "I found them."

TWENTY-NINE

"Tell me what happened to Glen," said the driver.

"What?"

They were back in the coach now, heading for the final destination on day three of their trip. Jack chose to sit with the driver again. They had unfinished business.

"Tell me," the driver repeated. "You've not said. I know he was a D-Day paradog. But I don't know what happened to him."

Jack coughed. He was worried he would cry again. "I don't really want to talk about it," he said.

"Look, Jack," the driver said. "Museums and

trips like this are about us learning what happened and then passing that message on to others, so that war doesn't have to happen so much. I know you get that now. So pass it on. You have a duty. Tell me what happened to Glen."

Jack could remember everything he had read in the library book. Every word. Every detail. He'd spent days trying not to think about it, trying not to imagine doing the same thing to Finn.

But now?

It was weird. Now the driver had said what he had said, Jack felt a huge need to tell the story and share what he had learned.

"After he threw Glen out of the plane, Corteil jumped as well. He'd put a light on Glen's harness so he could follow him down. They landed. It was dark. It was hard to judge what they were landing on. Some paratroopers landed in fields the Germans had flooded. Several men drowned, suffocated under their parachutes."

"But not Corteil and Glen?" the driver asked.

"No. They landed in marshy fields. Flooded, but not deep water. But they were still a long way from where they should have been. They had these clicker things to communicate. They sounded a bit like insects and it was a way of knowing you had friends, not enemies, around you."

"So they formed a small group?" the driver asked.

"Yes. The main officer gathered all the men he could find and led them to a narrow track with hedges on either side. It was dead quiet. They had no idea where the enemy troops would be. Corteil was at the front with Glen. Glen was sniffing the air, smelling out the Germans. That was his job. Different nationalities smell different. It's because of what you eat, what you wear, what you use to wash. Everything and anything—"

"Good. Tell me what happened, Jack," the driver said.

"And Glen was supposed to sniff out mines too – bombs buried underground, which would go off if you trod on them."

"Right."

"The Allies were dropping bombs on the beaches before dawn," Jack said, "making it harder for the Germans to defend them. And fighter planes were searching the area around the beaches for enemy troops and may have mistaken Corteil's group for Germans. Glen heard them first. He stood still, so Corteil knew he had heard something. Corteil put his arm up and the men behind him squatted, expecting to be shot at. Then they heard the planes coming. The men tried to scatter off the track, because they knew what was coming, but they couldn't escape because the hedgerows were too thick."

Jack stopped and watched the driver swallow, eyes fixed on the road as he drove.

"And," Jack took a deep breath, "half of the men were killed by friendly fire. Glen and Corteil died instantly."

"I see," the driver said, dropping down a gear as he prepared to turn the bus right, into a village called Ranville.

"There's one more thing," Jack sniffed.

"Tell me."

"They found Corteil with his hand still gripping Glen's lead. They were still together even after they were killed ..."

The coach had stopped.

"Where are we?" Jack coughed.

“Ranville Cemetery,” the driver said.

“Right.” Jack felt exhausted.

“Listen, Jack,” the driver said. “You told that story well. You know what I said about coming to places like this and the museum and hearing stories about the past – how it is important to help us to understand?”

“Yeah?”

“Well, you’ve done it with your story. You’ve told a story that is sad. Terrible things happening to a young man and a dog. But you’ve shown how brave they were, how they were trying to do the right thing. Emile was doing it to help liberate his father’s homeland. He was doing it for a good reason. Trying to defeat the Nazis. And together they helped get the job done. They played a part in the liberation of France. Even though it cost them their lives.”

Jack nodded. He was suddenly flooded with a

feeling of pride. He was proud of Corteil as well as Glen. He felt close to them. Connected to them. And now he had a deep desire to pay his respects to Corteil.

Jack fumbled with his folder to take out his cross. He put his hand inside.

It wasn't there.

Jack tipped his folder upside down onto his lap, checked each booklet and piece of paper, searching for his cross. He hadn't wanted to plant the cross at Corteil's grave, but now, after everything he had seen and learned in Normandy, it felt really important to do so. But the cross had gone.

"What is it?" the driver asked.

"Nothing." Jack shrugged and climbed off the bus.

THIRTY

Year 6 stood at the entrance to Ranville Cemetery. It was a bright but cool evening. The stone arch at the entrance was in shadow, but beyond it, among hundreds of graves, a tall marble cross was illuminated by the evening sun.

"OK." Mr Salah was speaking. "Ranville Cemetery. This is our last stop. Then we have a short drive to the ferry port. OK?"

"Yes, sir," Year 6 said as one.

"We will have one hour here, where each of you can go and find your soldier's grave and plant your cross. Then I will lead a short service of remembrance. Then we must go. Our ferry leaves in three hours."

Jack looked at all his classmates clutching their crosses, some of them appearing emotional. After he let them all go ahead of him, Jack stumbled through a tall marble gateway with a short wall on either side. On one side of the wall was a stone into which the words RANVILLE WAR CEMETERY were neatly carved.

Ahead was a block of white gravestones, each about a metre high, in rows and columns. All set in lush green lawns. The cemetery was surrounded by trees.

Walking behind Lucas, Jack read the gravestones as they moved past them.

D.R. Hurley. Parachute regiment. Age 19.

One of the bravest. One of the best.

R.F. Johns. Parachute Regiment. Age 24.

He died as he lived, fearless.

P.G. Sampson. Age 21. Our son gave his life

to make the world a better place.

Jack felt terrible. He read the last one again. *Our son gave his life to make the world a better place.* It was true. Jack knew it was true. He felt a tear tickle his cheek. He looked out across the cemetery and saw single children or small groups squatting at different graves. He could hear the soft murmur of their voices reading the inscriptions.

Jack walked with Lucas, who quickly found the grave he was looking for and planted his cross.

After a few minutes, Jack decided to join the others for the service, cursing himself for not looking after his cross. He was shocked now by the number of dead as he took in the size of the cemetery. Block after block of graves, two or three hundred in each block. There were thousands of graves. Jack stopped, just for a second, to get his head round the numbers – every one of these dead men had been somebody's son or even father – then carried on walking towards the centre.

Mr Salah was standing in a semi-circle with some of Year 6. Children read out letters written by soldiers during the war. Mrs Mace played the "Last Post" on her flute. All of this took place as the setting sun sent ripples of light through the leaves of a huge tree. Jack could smell cut grass.

Two pupils had been chosen to lay a wreath at the cross in the centre of the semi-circle of children. As they walked solemnly forwards, Jack noticed that Mr Salah was looking up at the sky, his jaw fixed as he tried to control his emotions.

Jack bowed his head, trying to breathe properly. His legs felt weak. He felt someone come up and stand next to him but he didn't turn round. It didn't seem right to do anything other than to look at the ground. He felt like a fool for not looking after his cross. He was desperate now to plant it.

Then he heard a voice.

THIRTY-ONE

"You dropped this back at school."

The bus driver handed Jack an envelope. "The grave is in the first block on the right."

Jack took the envelope and felt what was inside through the paper. A thin piece of wood in the shape of a cross.

Jack looked at the driver. He had his cross. He could place it on Corteil's grave.

"Thanks," he said, keeping his jaw tight, like Mr Salah.

The driver winked. "Listen, Corteil's not on his own in there. Glen's in the grave too."

Jack turned. Both of them? In the grave? Together? He felt himself smile. He walked a few paces, then stopped.

Jack could tell which grave it was. Four people stood around it, another kneeling. Corteil was one of the more well-known soldiers buried here. Because of his story. Because of Glen. If graves could be popular, this one was.

Jack waited until the people were ready to leave. He didn't want to plant his cross with anyone else around. Well, anyone except his friends.

Lucas and Kasandra stood with him as he waited, saying nothing. When all was clear, he walked briskly to the grave to find it had six crosses already planted in its dry soil. And flowers. And a photograph of Glen.

Jack read.

14410713 PRIVATE

E.S. CORTEIL

PARACHUTE REGIMENT

ARMY AIR CORPS

6TH JUNE 1944 AGE 19

HAD YOU KNOWN OUR BOY

YOU WOULD HAVE LOVED HIM TOO.

"GLEN" HIS PARATROOP DOG

WAS KILLED WITH HIM

Jack planted his cross, feeling the soil crumble easily as he pushed it into the ground. He wondered if he should say something. He'd seen films where people went to graves and spoke. But he didn't really know what to say. He coughed and stared at the ground, read the inscription at the bottom of the grave again. Coughed again.

He wanted to speak, just to say something. The graveyard was quiet, with the odd murmur of a voice. Otherwise there was only the sound of birds and of the wind rustling the branches and leaves.

"I'm sorry," Jack said. "For blaming you for ... you know ... for Glen. And I wanted to say thank you too. For doing what you did. Both of you."

Jack looked at Lucas and Kasandra. "Thank you too," he said.

His two friends smiled back at him.

"Now we have to go and plant Kasandra's cross," Lucas said. "Miss Khan said she would take us three over to the graveyard next to the church." Lucas took Kasandra's hand and led her to his support teacher.

Jack followed.

THIRTY-TWO

In the coach on the way to the ferry terminal Jack was allowed to go back and sit with Lucas and Kasandra.

As they sat and chatted, Jack felt his phone buzz in his pocket. It was a photo of Finn with his mum. There was a lake in the background. There was no way it could be a selfie.

Jack smiled.

His mum and dad must be together. Probably. What did that mean? Were they OK now? Had they sorted everything out like they promised they would? And what had Dad decided to do?

Jack frowned. He couldn't wait to see his dad now. To tell him about the trip. To hear whether he'd decided to go to Afghanistan or not.

*

Back in England, Jack asked Mr Salah if he could sit up front on the coach for the last hour of the journey. He wanted to talk to the driver, ask him more about what it had been like being a paratrooper. It meant that when the bus turned into the school car park at seven o'clock that evening, Jack was well placed to see all the parents waiting.

He saw Lucas's mum first, wringing her hands like she had been when they'd left. He saw Kasandra's mum in her green headscarf, her eyes glistening.

Then he saw his mum. She was on her tiptoes, staring along the top deck of the coach as it drew up.

Jack looked at the ground by his mum. Emerging from the forest of feet was Finn.

Not panicking. Not pulling on his lead. Not thrashing from side to side like he had been when they left. He was staring directly at Jack, eyes locked, tail wagging.

Then suddenly he was pulling, almost snatching the lead out of Mum's hand.

Jack grinned. "Seen my dog?" he said to the driver.

The driver laughed. "He almost pulled your dad's hand off."

"What?" Jack said.

"Your dad's hand. He almost pulled it off. Sorry ... that is your dad, right?"

Jack looked again. The hand that was holding Finn's lead could not be his mum's, as she was waving both her hands up at the children above.

"It is," Jack said, a grin widening on his face.

Jack couldn't believe it. He'd hoped for it but not expected it. He felt sure now that whatever decision his dad had made about Afghanistan, his family would stay together, and that was the most important thing.

The driver pulled his handbrake on and nodded at Jack.

"Jump off. Looks like your dog needs to see you."

Jack looked to see Finn scrabbling at the door. He could hear his sharp barks now. Jack pulled the door open to be met by a frenzy of paws and fur and his dog's mouth chewing his hands, then going for his ears.

Jack took control of Finn and remembered to turn to the driver.

"Thanks," Jack said.

EMILE CORTEIL AND GLEN IN 1944

SOME QUESTIONS ABOUT *D-DAY DOG* AND WAR

Here are some questions about some of the issues that come up in *D-Day Dog*. Can you answer them? Then ask yourself about the reasons for your answer. Is there someone else in your class at school or at home that thinks differently? It might be interesting to talk to them about the differences in your opinions. There are no right or wrong answers, but these are important issues to think about.

- In *D-Day Dog* Jack thinks that playing video games about war is exciting. Why do you think that some people find war video games exciting?

- When Jack visits the grave of Emile Corteil and Glen, he says thank you to them. Have you ever visited a soldier's grave or a memorial? Would you say thank you? What would you be saying thank you for?

- Jack is proud his dad is a Reserve soldier. Would you be proud if someone in your family was – or had been – a soldier?

- On the Animals in War Memorial in London there is a sentence carved into the stone. It says "They had no choice". Because they have no choice, do you think it is ever acceptable for animals to be used in war?

- Why do you think that a lot of people chose to become soldiers and fight against Hitler in the Second World War?

- The D-Day soldiers gave their tomorrow so we could have our today. Do you think that was the right thing for the soldiers to do?

- Kasandra wanted her city in Syria to be liberated like the French were on D-Day. Do you think war can be justified if its aim is to liberate innocent civilians?

- "Collateral damage" is a phrase used to describe people who are killed when they accidentally get caught up in a war. Do you think that collateral damage is ever an acceptable cost of war?

- Glen and Emile Corteil were killed accidentally by their own side in a friendly-fire incident. What do you think of the term "friendly fire"?

- When the children visit the beach where thousands of American soldiers were killed, do you think it is right that they play football there?

FIND OUT MORE ABOUT D-DAY AND NORMANDY

While he was writing *D-Day Dog*, Tom Palmer visited all of the locations in Normandy that Jack and his schoolmates go to in the book. Doing this kind of research helps Tom make sure he gets his descriptions of the places exactly right. But it also gives him a sense of the history that underlies what he is writing about.

Once he'd written the book, Tom went back to Normandy to make a series of short films about the places Jack visits and where Emile and Glen landed, in which he explains how and why he goes about writing stories about real historic events.

You can watch the films – and find more free resources – by visiting:

www.tompalmer.co.uk/dday-dog

ANIMALS IN WAR

It is well known that animals of all kinds played a vital part in the First and Second World Wars, but this was not a new phenomenon. Animals have been used in human warfare throughout history, as these few examples show.

AD 60 HORSES AND DOGS

Boudica, the British queen who so nearly defeated the might of the Roman Empire, was such a problem to the Mediterranean occupiers because she involved horses and dogs alongside men and women on the battlefield. Horses were used to pull light chariots to deliver male and female warriors to the heart of the battle. Huge dogs were tasked with ripping Roman cavalry from the backs of their horses, so that the Iron Age foot soldiers could finish them off on the ground.

1916 DOGS AND PIGEONS

During the Battle of Verdun – the longest battle of the First World War, which resulted in nearly 800,000 casualties – a group of French soldiers were running out of ammunition and seemingly doomed. Then a popular messenger dog called Satan was seen to be almost flying across the battlefield, until he was hit by a hail of bullets. Despite his injuries, when called by his owner, Satan dragged his dying body to his master's side, delivering a message telling the embattled French to hold on because reinforcements were on their way. Satan was also carrying two pigeons in a small basket on his back. The pigeons were then released, carrying a message to tell French reinforcements the location of the German gun positions, helping to save the town. Of the three animals, one pigeon survived, one died and sadly the loyal dog died too.

1949 SHIP'S CAT

The only feline to be awarded the Dickin Medal was the ship's cat of HMS *Amethyst*. Although he was badly injured in the Yangtze Incident during the Chinese Civil War, Simon the cat took up a post in the ship's mess, where food was kept and served. He killed dozens of rats who had infested the ship after it was shelled, securing the meagre food supply for the surviving sailors and also helping to keep up their morale.

1953 SERGEANT RECKLESS

Reckless was the only horse in American military history to be awarded the rank of sergeant. She played an important part in the Korean War, particularly during the Battle of Outpost Vegas, when she made 51 trips to resupply the beleaguered US soldiers at the front with ammunition. After making her deliveries, she also carried two injured soldiers to safety, despite being wounded twice herself. The soldiers she served with loved her so much that some of them threw their flak jackets over Reckless to protect her from incoming fire.

THE DICKIN MEDAL

The PDSA Dickin Medal has been awarded to 71 animals between 1943 and 2019 to acknowledge their bravery or devotion to duty in war. The first three medals were awarded to recognise the role three pigeons played in helping to rescue different stranded air crews. Since then, 34 dogs, 29 pigeons, 4 horses and 1 cat have been awarded the Dickin Medal. In addition, an honorary medal was awarded to pay tribute to all the animals that served in the First World War.

D-DAY
DOG

ANIMALS IN WAR MEMORIAL

On Park Lane in London you can visit the Animals in War Memorial. It is made up of a high curving wall that portrays images of animals sculpted into the surface of the stone, as well as bronze statues of two mules, a horse and a dog.

The main inscription on the stone reads:

THIS MONUMENT IS DEDICATED TO ALL THE ANIMALS THAT SERVED AND DIED ALONGSIDE BRITISH AND ALLIED FORCES IN WARS AND CAMPAIGNS THROUGHOUT TIME

Carved into the stone on the far end of the memorial are the words "They had no choice".

If you find yourself in London, the memorial is very near Hyde Park and Oxford Street and can be reached by tube, bus and on foot. It is well worth a visit.

www.animalsinwar.org.uk

ACKNOWLEDGEMENTS

This book is about the men, women and children who gave their tomorrow so we could have our today. Without that sacrifice we might be living in a very different world. My first thank you should be to them and to the animals that served with them.

Thank you too to my editor – Ailsa Bathgate – for being so patient and intelligent in the way she edited me. And to Victoria Walsh for her editorial work too. Thank you to everyone at Barrington Stoke for being such a great publisher to write for. Thank you also to my agent – David Luxton – and his colleagues for making the book possible.

I would like to say a big thank you to my many manuscript readers – Simon Robinson, Simon Hinchliffe, Alison Brumwell, Rebecca Palmer, Iris Palmer, Charles Little and Jim Sells – who all contributed their different views and expertise to help make the book better.

I devised, researched and planned this book with the help of Year 6 and the teachers at Ashville College in Harrogate – in the classroom and while actually travelling with them to Normandy. The book is dedicated to the school as a thank you for their generosity and openness.

My final thanks go to the driver of the bus on the school trip – for driving us, talking to me and telling me about what he did in 1982. And to Emile Servais Corteil and his paradog, Glen.

978-1-78112-586-1

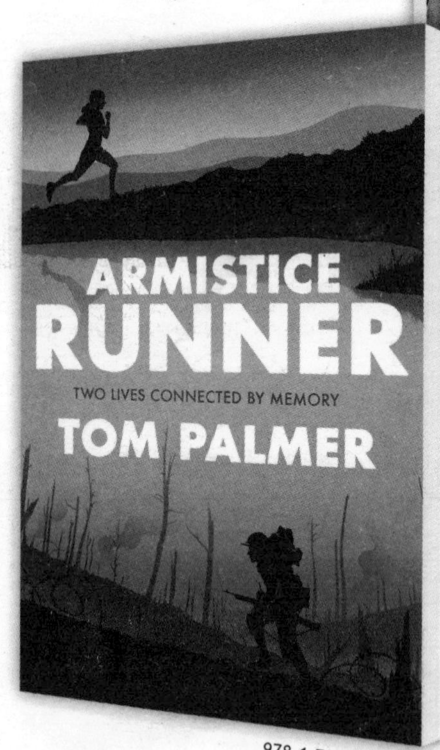

978-1-78112-825-1

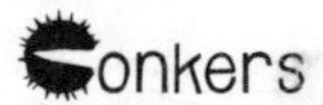